# Praise for the *St. Nacho's* Series
# by Z. A. Maxfield

### *St. Nacho's*

"I found this story of love, hope, and redemption absolutely stunning and enthusiastically endorse it as a Recommended Read. *St Nacho's* is without a doubt one of the better books I have read in quite a while."

– Whitney, *Fallen Angel Reviews*

"*St. Nacho's* is by far one of the most entrancing and emotional romances I've read in a long time and Z.A. Maxfield has certainly cemented her place in the keeper shelf of all m/m fans that like their characters with depth of emotion along with bone-melting sex!"

– Sabella, *Joyfully Reviewed*

### *Physical Therapy*

"This is a profound and beautifully written novel full of strong emotions and vibrant descriptions. I highly recommend it."

– Christina, *Romance Junkies*

"*Physical Therapy* is a clear example of how the underdog can always rise up, that love takes no prisoners or excuses, and true friends love you unconditionally. If you enjoyed *St. Nacho's*, you don't want to miss this fantastic sequel."

– *Literary Nymphs*

# Loose Id®

ISBN 13: 978-1-60737-417-6
PHYSICAL THERAPY
Copyright © December 2009 by Z. A. Maxfield
Originally released in e-book format in May 2009

Cover Art by Anne Cain
Cover Layout and Design by April Martinez

**DISCLAIMER:** Many of the acts described in our BDSM/fetish titles can be dangerous. Please do not try any new sexual practice, whether it be fire, rope, or whip play, without the guidance of an experienced practitioner. Neither Loose Id nor its authors will be responsible for any loss, harm, injury or death resulting from use of the information contained in any of its titles.

This book is an original publication of Loose Id. Each individual story herein was previously published in e-book format only by Loose Id and is a work of fiction. Any similarity to actual persons, events or existing locations is entirely coincidental.

Printed in the U.S.A. by
Lightning Source, Inc.
1246 Heil Quaker Blvd
La Vergne TN 37086
www.lightningsource.com

# PHYSICAL THERAPY

# Dedication

*For my mom, whose journey into homeopathy, massage, and acupressure made me the weirdest kid on the block for all the right reasons. YOU ROCK.*

*1/5/1925-4/28/2009*

# Chapter One

The windshield wipers on my old Honda slapped in time to the music on the radio, such an eerie coincidence that I changed radio stations, going to one after another, finally settling on a jazz radio station playing a soft blues piece. As the droplets merged, they formed rivulets, gathered together, and ran in slashes down the glass beneath the inadequate light. Slowing to a crawl alongside the black skeleton of a wooden pier, I stopped the car and got out, hardly aware that the rain came down and lashed at my clothing.

The pier was long, dark, and deserted. Its pilings groaned against the rushing water as it flowed and swirled around them. It seemed to me the pier was standing uncertainly, like a dog watching in horror as water sucks and pulls at the sand beneath its paws when a wave recedes. I often froze and felt my own feet being sucked out from under me these days.

For the first time in almost a year, my hands itched for a cigarette; I could almost feel it there between my fingers, like a phantom limb. I started off walking, the battered structure drawing me closer by the sheer enormity of its desolation.

From where I stood by the pier, I could see the waterfront businesses in tiny Santo Ignacio. The lights were out now, at this hour of the morning. I'd made my decision to come to Santo Ignacio late that afternoon, impulsively thrown everything I owned into a few boxes and bags, said good-bye to my roommate, and driven off. I'd always known I'd end up here. I just never knew when I'd finally decide it was time to come.

I had arrived at almost eleven p.m. and checked into my dreary motel room, falling onto the bed and into a deep sleep almost immediately. I'd slept for a little over two hours but then woke up fully refreshed, eager to get a look at this tiny seaside town.

Now, at close to three in the morning, I was the only living thing stirring for miles. I crunched across the sand in hiking boots, just a little way, until I could make out the unlit sign for Nacho's Bar, where my friend Cooper worked. It gave me a sense of satisfaction to see it, not that I'd return during the day when it was inhabited. I just... It felt good knowing the place that Cooper had told me about was there. I was glad to know it really existed. That I'd found it.

My cell phone burned in my pocket. I wouldn't call Cooper, because Cooper was happy and healthy. Cooper had moved on with his life and his new lover, Shawn. It wouldn't be easy to tell Cooper I was here in town, because there was so much about me that he wouldn't understand.

First and most important, that I wasn't here to get Cooper back. I would hardly be able to convince Cooper of that fact, though, and didn't care to try. I hadn't left a trail of truth in my wake at the best of times, and Cooper had seen me at my worst. When Cooper found out I was in Santo Ignacio, he would believe I was here for him. That I wasn't over him, that I was still blaming him for the accident in our past, that I wasn't better at all. That I hadn't thrown the

But ever since Izzie lost her last helper, Jake, she's been too busy for us."

"Jake?" I asked. Maybe I could get some information about what Izzie expected from her employees. "How come he left?"

"Jake was a sweet boy," sighed one of the oldest ladies, who had short silvery hair that was fluffed up in front and cut very close, almost like a man's, in the back. "He left us to go off to Stanford," she said. "He was glad to be going, but I think he was already feeling homesick."

"That's right," said Sally. "Izzie said his aura was positively puce when he took his things and said good-bye."

They all nodded at one another.

"Can Izzie really see auras?" I asked.

"Oh yes." Sally spoke up before anyone had a chance. "It's documented in the paper that she tried to tell the previous mayor to slow his schedule down. Poor man."

"He died?" I whispered.

"No," said Sally. "Of course not, but his wife left him the following week after he was caught in flagrante delicto with the housekeeper."

I felt like shaking my head. Like it would make that noise that happens when cartoon characters were snapping back into shape. "She saw it in his aura?"

"Oh no, dear," said my soft-spoken lady with the kind brown eyes. "In the housekeeper's."

Sally was nodding sagely. "Izzie can always tell when someone is"—she looked around and lowered her voice—"getting some."

The puffy silver-haired lady snorted. "That's why we don't come in on Monday mornings."

I felt my eyebrows fly up until I was sure my hair hid them. "She can really…?"

"If it's recent," said Sally, whose eyes seemed to be dancing with enjoyment at my discomfort. "Poor Jake. He learned the hard way not to—"

"Don't be telling tales, Sally." My brown-haired lady looked back at me. "Still, it's probably best *you* don't find out the hard way."

"I guess not," I said. We all stared at each other for a while. "You ladies are going to be a handful, aren't you?"

"Probably," said Sally, looking at the stack of files I had on the floor in front of me. "What should we start with?"

"How about names?" I asked, and they all started talking at once. There were six of them, and I decided to take matters into my own hands by grabbing the top file on the stack. "Ann," I read. "Who is Ann?"

The brown-haired lady waved her hand at me. "Me."

"How about you and I get started on curls?"

She smiled and followed me to the machine, taking up her position after adjusting the seat. One by one, I led them to machines, giving them light instructions and adding weight or reps if something seemed too easy. Mostly it was like herding cats, and even I was tired by the time they were done an hour later. They came out of the ladies' locker room in purple clothing and big red hats that made them look like tropical birds. I loved them. I was already enjoying my new job.

They were trying to get Izzie to give up what my aura told her when another customer entered the gym. I was still laughing at something they were saying when I caught sight of him.

He was big; it seemed he almost filled the doorway with his presence, and it didn't help that he had Lofstrand crutches, the kind that wrap around your forearms with a handle that sticks out for you to lean on when you take a step. He took one cautious step into the building and then another, and it seemed hard for him. His coordination was all wrong, and I suspected that he'd had a head injury, maybe, or some damage to his spinal cord because he was wearing shorts and I couldn't see any scarring on his legs. He led with his crutches, giving himself ample time to set them steadily before taking each step.

My ladies moved back for him, silent and sad. It seemed almost like a funeral procession. I didn't understand the atmosphere at all; it had changed so quickly. Izzie greeted the newcomer quietly and led him back into the gym. I couldn't hear what she said, but as soon as the two of them were out of earshot, to a man—or a woman as the case may be—my ladies seemed to sigh.

"What?" I asked. I was determined to find out as much as I could from this small gold mine of information in the form of cheerful older women.

"That's Ken Ashton," Sally said in a theatrical whisper, as if I should know what she meant.

"He was in a terrible accident," Ann added.

Sally nodded. "He was the best ballplayer this town ever produced. A senior at Cal State Fullerton when he had the accident. They have a great program for baseball, and we all had such high hopes for him. That was almost six months ago."

"It was a terrible shame. His girlfriend didn't make it." Ann spoke so low I barely heard her. They all looked in the direction that Ashton had gone with Izzie.

"What does he do here?" I asked.

"Izzie's been working with him since he first came home from the hospital. That's been what, two months?" She looked around. "His coordination was…"

"I see," I said. There was a strained silence until Ann broke it.

"He's much better now. The doctors are hopeful he'll make a nearly complete recovery."

"That's good." I doubted that even if his body came back 100 percent he'd ever recover completely. There was something about being brushed by tragedy that marked a person forever. I had seen that in his eyes when he'd glanced my way in passing. They'd been unbelievably attractive; light blue with black rings around them, surrounded by lashes like a girl's, but they'd held no life in them, no spark. "Poor man." I was only aware I'd said that aloud when the Red Hats bobbed their silent agreement.

I held the door while the ladies exited, giving them a cheerful wave as they argued about driving or walking and breakfast or lunch, and then I went back inside. The door closed behind me with a sigh. It seemed eerily quiet as I walked back into the gym area. I thought I'd grab some disinfectant wipes and do the machine handles. Places where people touched. I was going through Izzie's basket of supplies when I heard her voice behind me.

"Jordan." She waved me over. "I wonder if you could come in here a moment." I headed toward the therapy room where she stood, still holding the wipes in my hand. "There's someone I'd like you to meet."

I followed her into the small room, which she kept dimly lit and silent. Ken Ashton was walking on a treadmill. He moved slowly, both hands gripping the support bars.

"Ken." Izzie went to him and turned off the treadmill. As it slowed to a crawl, he looked relieved, and I could see he was tight and white about the mouth, as if he'd been concentrating fiercely. He had beads of sweat popping out on his brow, and he heaved a sigh when the conveyor belt finally ground to a halt. He turned and removed earbuds from his ears, flipping the wire neatly around his neck. "I would like you to meet Jordan. He's my new assistant, and he's going to be able to do massage for you after your workouts."

I held out my hand and dipped my head. "Ken, nice to meet you." It was hard somehow to look at him. It was like looking at the scene of a bomb blast, when people are still reeling with shock as they're crawling out of the rubble. He peered at the world as if through a veil of smoky haze and wreckage, still stunned in the aftermath of his disaster.

"Jordan." He acknowledged me in a clipped kind of way. I thought maybe he resented the intrusion. Maybe he wanted to be left alone.

"Well," I began. "I can come back when you're ready for a massage, if you like."

"It will be good for you," said Izzie. "He'll help you to lengthen and relax the muscles that get tight when I put you through your paces."

"I don't know that my insurance will cover it," he said, no longer looking at me.

I glanced at Izzie, who seemed to be trying to tell me something with her eyes. "I don't know what Jordan even charges yet," she told him, running one of her leathery hands over his shoulder. He pulled away from her touch.

"Hey," I said. "No problem, I'm like a dealer; I know once you've tried me out, you'll be hooked. The first one's always free."

Ken turned away and started to towel off with some difficulty as he leaned against the table. "Maybe later. Get him out of here, Izzie."

My mouth hung open in shock, but I only stood there for a moment before Izzie was gently leading me out the door.

"What did I say?" I asked her. I couldn't imagine that what I'd said was so offensive he'd have me thrown out. Turn down a free massage. *Who turns down a free massage?*

"It's all right," Izzie said under her breath. "He's all right. He's...bitter. He just..." She looked behind her into the room. I could see Ken struggling to retrieve his crutches and put on his jacket. Izzie sighed. "He's embarrassed because he's still awkward. He was in an accident; hit by a drunk driver. His girlfriend was killed."

I pulled her out of the doorway, and the door shut automatically behind her. "What on earth are you thinking?

I told you about me! I'm the last person you should introduce to him. He won't want me touching him. He won't even want me living in St. Nacho's."

"Well, it's not up to him, is it?"

I shook my head. "What?"

"I read your résumé. You've done your time. And more importantly, I think…"

"What?" I asked again after she trailed off.

"More importantly, I think you may have something to offer him."

"I *offered* him a free massage," I said. "He declined."

She cuffed my arm lightly to let me know I wasn't funny. "I know you don't believe me, but I want you to try again, and keep trying, until you get him to talk to you." For once her severe expression made sense. "And since you're giving him a massage for free, I'll give *you* this for free," she said. "Your auras are exactly the same. Exactly. I'll draw a picture later and show you what I mean."

The door opened behind us and Ken came through it. He didn't meet either of our eyes.

"Excuse me," he said politely. Izzie raised her brows and turned to him.

"Where do you think you're going?" she asked him. He couldn't seem to find an answer. "You still have free weights, and I don't care what you say, you will let Jordan give you a quick massage at the end of your workout."

"But—"

Izzie laughed, and it kind of sounded metallic and silvery, completely at odds with her bulky and leathery body. In a tone that said she had plans if he didn't comply, she said, "When have I ever listened to your excuses? Now, move."

He turned around then, shoulders slumped, looking smaller than he had coming out. I could see how Izzie might wilt a man, and Ken was definitely wilted. He was still enormous, even compared to Izzie, and either the door wasn't exactly regulation size or I'd misjudged his height when he came in because he almost, *almost* had to duck.

"Call me when you need me," I said as Izzie was about to close the door behind them. She met my eyes and nodded.

"*Damn*," I whispered to myself. I'd left home and traveled two thousand miles to get away from a town that reviled me as a drunken killer. And now, whether I liked it or not, I was about to get up close and personal with a man who had every reason to hate me for the same thing.

That was fucking irony for you, right there.

# Chapter Three

I'd eradicated the cold and flu germs on the handholds of most of the large equipment when Izzie motioned me back toward the therapy room. I had to like her; she had a hiring policy that I was benefiting from, but she seemed to have another policy, one of trial by fire, that was making me nervous.

Her eyes, as they met mine when I walked into the therapy room, probably said an awful lot of things I couldn't read because I didn't know her well enough. Ken was lying chest down on a portable massage table, wearing only his shorts. His body was still and his head was turned away. I was looking at him when I heard Izzie close the door softly behind her. We were alone.

Massage is an unusual choice for a man like me because it requires that you remain silent with most of your clients, and I'm normally a very talkative guy. Cooper always accused me of wanting to be the center of attention and never shutting up, even when it was in my best interest. While age and—possibly—maturity made me less likely to blurt out whatever was on my mind these days, I'd found that caring for another person physically, touching their skin, smoothing knotted muscles, pushing and pulling on the very stuff of which people are made, brought a kind of contemplative, content silence that I for once didn't have to fill.

No one was more surprised by this than I was.

I went to work. "I wonder if it would be all right if we began with you faceup," I murmured in a voice I'd cultivated just for this purpose, something between graveyard shift jazz disc jockey and grief counselor. "I'd like to finish off with the large muscles in your back. Unless... I mean, if you have sinus trouble or back problems and have trouble resting in a facedown position and then getting up..."

"No, facedown or faceup, either way," he replied. He didn't seem to be looking forward to this as much as some clients did. He began the awkward process of shifting from facedown to faceup on a wobbly table. I held it steady while he turned, and given his size and level of coordination, it wasn't easy. Wordlessly, I offered my arm to anchor him.

I found a pump bottle full of body lotion, a kind I liked that smelled like rosemary and eucalyptus, and put some on my hands to warm it. Neither Ken nor I spoke further, as I did his shoulders, arms, and pecs. I focused on his hands, partly because it seemed to relax him, and partly because they were callused from using the crutches, and it seemed to me his forearms and hands were probably bearing a lot of his weight. I knew just from manipulating his arms that his shoulders would be stretched so taut it might even hurt him for me to work on them.

"Tell me if the pressure I use here, or anywhere at all, is too uncomfortable," I told him, as I used my thumbs on the palms of his hands and gently stretched them open.

"It's fine," he said. His whole body was still tight and tense. So much so that his shoulders were drawn up toward his ears, and I realized that even if I was bringing tears to his eyes he probably wouldn't tell me. I had to look at his face for cues. I came around and did the other side, working silently and still watching him closely.

One of the first things my mother asked when I started learning massage techniques was what I thought about when I worked. My mom was my guinea pig, the first person I ever worked on, allowing me to practice on her even when I didn't know what I was doing, and was still reading aloud from muscle diagrams. I told her I mostly thought of things like how nice the person will feel when I'm done, or whether I'm managing to make them feel good when I rub their feet or hands.

It was a pleasure, back then, to go back home while my dad was at work and do something for my mother that she might have considered a luxury far beyond her reach. It was good to do something we didn't have to talk through.

She was always afraid that my father would find out and get angry, as if she weren't holding up her end of a marital bargain they had, as if she were indulging in some sort of frivolous and extravagant pastime while she should be darning his socks. Of all the things I hated about my family, the worst was leaving my mother in Wisconsin when I came out here to California. I felt bad about leaving her alone, because despite her thirty-year marriage to my father, my mother had always been alone.

Though I talked to her frequently, my mother continued to lead a fairly loveless life, and although she knew and understood why I had left, it felt a little like leaving her in a burning house, saving myself at her expense. I had to remind myself it was her choice to stay with my father every time I thought about it.

Ken must have been watching me closely as well because, just as I allowed the tiniest flicker of a frown, I heard his voice, almost hoarse and rusty with disuse, ask, "What goes through your head when you do that?"

"My head?" I asked, stalling for time. I wasn't going to talk about my family. "When I'm not thinking the names of the muscles, I'm imagining that I'm making you feel good."

"Hm," he grunted. I was working on the muscles around his forearms, which were knotted and stiff under my fingers like lumpy Play-Doh. He exhaled a deep sigh then, and I thought to myself, gotcha.

I continued to work, moving on to his legs; to the four muscles that make up the quadriceps and the muscles that wrap around the shinbone, although I usually work the calves from the back. I gave the same attention to his feet and ankles that I'd given his hands and wrists, stretching and smoothing the plantar fascia, and separating and pulling on his toes. Each toe was long and strong and had two or three dark hairs struggling out of the knuckles. It was a rather fine foot actually, for an athlete. I wondered if he'd ever had an injury to his feet or ankles; for such a jumbo-sized man they seemed to be rather slim and delicate.

As I did this, his legs fell open a little, his muscles relaxing as I soothed away the tension. I'd be lying if I said I wasn't attracted. He was beautiful, and I indulged for a brief second in the fantasy that he was *my* man and I was relaxing him as a prelude to making love.

I caught his eyes on me and looked down. I'm sure if the light had been better he'd have seen my face heat up.

I indicated without talking that he should turn over, again offering my arm. He rolled onto his stomach, and I started work on the backs of his legs. I often lose myself when I work, moving from one muscle group to the next, working my way in a pattern across the human body. If I've learned anything at all in the last few years, it might be that the body is a remarkable machine.

The human body can be strong and fluid, soft and pliable, hairy or smooth, scarred or pristine, young or old, and yet whatever shape it comes in, it's also capable of amazing feats of self-healing. That's what I was thinking about as I stroked the bulky trapezius and latissimus dorsi muscles along Ken's back and sides, when I felt the first tremors in the fine, large body beneath my hands.

Ken was crying.

That happened sometimes. It had happened to me once or twice when I was giving and getting massage in school. I had a friend in San Francisco where I interned who did acupressure and Reiki. Among the spiritual massage set, it wasn't uncommon to hear stories of emotional meltdown, and it happened to me frequently enough that I kept going, assuming he'd tell me to stop if he no longer wanted to feel my touch.

"Shit." He turned his face away then, pulling up his arms to hide it.

"It's all right," I told him. "Sometimes that happens."

Ken merely shook his head. For a while, he lay there, crying, and I continued, finishing up the imaginary grid on his body and coming around to finish with more soothing touches to his scalp. He was still trembling, I thought, although he made no sound. When I was done I left my hand on his shoulder and just waited for a while until his tears subsided. Afterward, he shook his head again, flexing his traps, the muscles of his broad shoulders, as if he could shake off his mood.

"I'd like to go get you some water to drink," I told him quietly. He looked up at me, frowning. "After a massage, it's really very important to hydrate."

"You sound like a funeral director."

I shrugged. "Wait here." I went out to ask Izzie if she had a plastic cup or something I could use to take Ken water.

She went to a back room and brought me a bottled water from some sort of mineral spring. "Here," she said. "There are always waters back there; feel free to get one whenever you need it.

"What do I owe you?" I asked, putting a hand to my back pocket for my wallet.

"Nothing. If it's for you or your clients, just take one."

I grinned. The last gym I worked in had charged me two-fifty a bottle and made me pay for the water I gave my clients. "Thanks." I returned to the therapy room and found Ken awkwardly putting on his shirt.

"Here," I said, holding out the water. He must have thought I was going to try to help him dress because he snapped at me.

"I can still dress myself."

"I was..." I held out the water when he looked up. "Here's your water."

Ken cleared his throat. "Sorry," he muttered, looking at the floor.

He was slipping his arms through the sleeves of a dark blue and tan Hawaiian shirt, pulling it closed over strong muscles and skin that was firm but pale. Crisp dark hair whorled around pink nipples. His neck still had the ghost of a tan where it met the collar of his shirt. When I looked at his face, his eyes were red and puffy, and he didn't seem to know where they should land.

"Thank you," he said. "Sorry, I—"

"No worries," I told him.

"I'll get out of your hair." He turned away.

"Seriously, Ken. There's nothing to be embarrassed about; that happens to a lot of people."

"Not to me." He started for the door.

I put a hand on his arm to stop him. "People really do have emotional responses to massage. It isn't uncommon."

"I thought you were just saying that." He slumped back down onto the massage table and let out a breath. "You're the first person I've met since the accident that I don't mind touching me."

"Me?" That was odd.

"I find you... People are touching me all the time. It's like I'm a slab of beef they're preparing for a meal. They make me nervous and angry. I find you...peaceful."

I snorted. "Okay, I *know* you're the first person who's ever called me peaceful." I sat down on a stool near him, letting him know that he wasn't odd for his reaction and supporting him through the aftermath as best I could.

For a minute, he seemed content to sit there with me in silence. I watched an amazing number of emotions play over his handsome face, most of which I couldn't begin to decipher. It was a good face—intelligent and open—and I tried very hard not to succumb to my attraction to it.

"Have you ever met anyone and right away you thought you'd like to spend time with them? Like they were tranquil water and you wanted to dive in? The minute you put your hands on me—"

I still had my hand on his arm, and I tried not to jerk it away. "*Whoa*. You don't know anything about me, Ken," I warned him. "I'm not who you think I am."

Izzie might not be happy about it, but I decided that whether she liked it or not, Ken deserved to be told about my past. I had the strongest feeling that if I didn't tell him— if he revealed any more of himself—he would feel betrayed. If I told him about myself—about the accident—and he left and never spoke to me again, so be it. Better that than him thinking I was hiding something.

"Look," I said. "There's something you need to know. I really want to help you, and I think I have something to offer you as you recover from your accident. But if you find out later rather than sooner, I think you'll—"

"Izzie told me you're gay," he interrupted. "If that's what this is about, I don't have a problem with that."

I was speechless for a minute. "No. That's not it." *Why had she told him that?* "No. I was in an accident."

"You too?" He pulled back and looked me over as though trying to see where I'd been injured.

"Yes, but... I mean..." I closed my eyes. It never, *ever* got easier. "This is so fucking hard. I was the *cause* of the accident, Ken. I was drunk. I cost someone their life. *I'm* the reason someone is grieving for a child. I went to jail for it."

It was as if he couldn't comprehend it, but when he finally did, he blew out a breath. "You?"

"Yes."

He yanked his arm away from me. "You fucking bastard. Mr. Compassion."

While not unexpected, a man of his size barking at me like that in an enclosed space was a lot to take in. I backed up against the door. "What the hell—"

He held his body rigid as he looked me over contemptuously. "So now you're out, and it's over? You've done your time and you can move on, and we're all supposed to play like nothing ever happened? How does that feel, to start over with a new slate after *you killed someone?*"

"How do you think?" I tried to keep my voice down. "How do you fucking *think* it feels?"

"I think it must feel a helluva lot better than waking up from a coma and remembering your best friend is dead."

I closed my eyes. "I imagine it does." I spoke so softly I doubted he heard me over his agitated breathing.

"And now you're what? Giving free massages? Pretending to know what people are going through? Giving advice?"

"That's not what this is. I just want to help. I'm sorry, Ken."

"Damn fucking straight you're sorry. For a minute, I could remember what it was like to feel again." He put his head in his hands. "It was like being human. I've felt like *meat* for so long."

Ken was breathing as though he'd run a mile. I swallowed hard. "What do you mean 'meat'?"

"I was conscious for a few minutes while they cut us out of the car. My friend Amy was dead. Staring. Her chest had been crushed. She... I'll never forget it. I realized then we're only meat."

"We're more than just that." But I knew. *I knew exactly what he meant.* There were people who never find that out, but I wasn't one of them.

"But when it's all over, that's all that's left, isn't it? Since then, I feel like walking meat." I couldn't begin to know what to say to that. He rubbed his eyes with the heels of both hands, looking so tired my heart broke for him. "I've been so angry. I've made everyone who ever loved me miserable, and here you come along, the embodiment of everything I hate, and you're the one person I'm drawn to."

"I can help you, if you'll let me," I tried approaching him and put a hand back on his arm.

He pulled away again, but not as far.

I kept talking. "I'm the worst person for you to turn to. I know that. But I'd like to do whatever I can."

"Are you doing this to make some sort of restitution?"

"If that were even possible—which it's not—it would take a lot more than a few massages to do it."

He exhaled a deep breath and stared at me for a long time. "Izzie told me not to be afraid of you."

"She did?" Izzie, *wow.* "Maybe you can tell me. Should I be afraid of Izzie?"

He sort of laughed a little, and it broke the tension just enough to relax the muscles in my body that were still urging me to get the hell out of town. "She's an unofficial aunt of mine, and no. She's really very nice." He slumped back on the massage table. "I thought I was over all of that crying shit."

I wondered if I should talk to him about it. "Sometimes I think that our bodies and our brains each store information about everything that happens to us. A friend of mine is afraid to get into a car because of an accident he had in the past. No amount of rational thinking helped. Whenever he even thought about getting into a car, he had these really bad panic attacks. He told himself it was fine, but his body just...went ballistic."

"What does that have to do this?" He may have just been asking where I was going with it. He may have thought I was nuts. His eyes gave away nothing.

"I wonder sometimes if our bodies hold on to things longer than our minds do, that's all. We can explain away something or rationalize it. Maybe we can be philosophical.

But our bodies just react." I stood quietly, wondering if Ken, who seemed to me at that moment like nothing so much as a big, sad bear, would have anything to say.

He put the bottle of water I gave him to his lips and drank about half of it down. I watched as his Adam's apple bobbed. He caught me looking and almost spilled. He wiped his mouth with the back of his hand, but just for a minute his lips glistened, wet and full. *Luscious.* I didn't know where that thought came from and pushed it as far away as I could.

"Maybe," he answered finally. "I don't know."

I shrugged. What could I say? Ken had been through an unspeakable tragedy of the very nature I had dealt to someone else. The thought worried me. He was a hot, hot man, and I felt the hard pull of attraction, but he was damaged in so many ways that I only had a little trouble turning any interest I might have had to compassion.

"Drinking water will help if you have any kind of dizziness or headache from the massage. Sometimes the lactic acid—"

"Got it," he said, taking up his crutches and heading for the door. When he finally had it open and was halfway through it, he looked back. "I've had some massages before, but yours was probably the best one, the most thorough I've ever had, and if it's possible, I think maybe Izzie's right. I should get them after my workouts."

I don't know why, but it felt like I was being picked first for the cool kids' basketball team at school or something. My heart did this little elated end-zone dance that I tried to tell myself had less to do with the blue eyes looking at me than the fact that Ken was a person who could really use my help.

That he trusted me to give it—despite my past—made me want to take a victory lap.

"Here you are." Izzie came up that moment and interrupted me. "What do you think, Ken? Did I do good hiring Jordan?"

"He's good with massage." Ken didn't seem eager to be put on the spot.

"That's nice to know." Izzie took his arm, looping her own under it above where his Lofstrand crutch gripped his forearm. "I'll work out the details with Jordan, and we'll see you next time. You say hello to your mom for me, all right?" She was stepping along with him, slowly, as he made his way to the front door. I watched the two of them go out to the parking lot together. There were only two people working out; obviously the morning rush in St. Nacho's was over. I wondered when I could expect another wave of people or if there would even be one.

Izzie returned from seeing Ken to his car. I asked her, "Does Ken drive or get a ride?"

"He drives." She looked at me speculatively. "Why?"

"I have a friend who had an accident and can't get into a car anymore." I didn't tell her that actually it had been the accident *I* caused, the car *I* was driving, that traumatized him.

"You made Ken Ashton cry." She frowned at me.

I felt awful. I know the blood must have drained from my face, and my heart sank. "I'm really sorry about that. He just—"

"He just what?" Izzie asked.

"He just...drained. Like I pulled a plug. I was doing his back, and he just... I'm sorry."

She shook her head. "Jordan, you crack me up." She caught me by the arm and pulled me back behind the counter. "That was probably the best thing that could have happened. I'm so delighted that I'm going to buy you lunch."

To say I was surprised would have been a whopping understatement. "What?"

"Look, when Ken came back here he hardly spoke to anyone. He's been staying with his family in the house where he grew up and he's just...frozen. You know what I mean?" She seemed to be going through a drawer full of take-out menus under the almost antique computer on the long check-in desk. Jumbles of notepads, pens, and sticky Post-it notes impeded her progress.

"Frozen?"

"Emotionally frozen. Spiritually drained. Lifeless. His mother's been so worried. I thought massage might help, but I never dreamed... Ah, here it is. Do you like noodle dishes?"

"Yeah, I guess." I was trying to think what kind of noodle dishes she might be talking about, but she had picked up the phone and was already telling someone she wanted two orders of chicken soft noodle.

I shook my head. "Vegetarian," I stage-whispered, pointing to myself.

"Make one of them a Buddha bowl," she told whoever was on the phone. "My new guy will come right over and get it. Thanks. Yeah, I have a new guy. His name is Jordan. Be

I hadn't looked at the schedule yet, but there were all kinds of dance classes at the gyms where I'd worked in San Francisco. I imagined my ladies of the Red Hat Society in some of the more daring fitness classes, like belly dancing or strip aerobics, and had to bite back a laugh. I had the feeling they would have gotten into the spirit of that just fine. They came over with their file folders then, all in a clump, and they reminded me of little girls in school.

I still couldn't put my finger on it, but things touched me in a strange way these days. Things appeared to me to be either crystal clear or completely obscure. I made connections in my mind that I never made before, like thinking of these ladies as little girls, and it made me glad to be able to help them out, to give them a little attention, because maybe that's what we all need sometimes.

There seemed to be some sort of private room behind the wall that held the men's locker room as well, which had a solid door and a sign that read THERAPY. Maybe that was where I would do massage, or maybe that's where Izzie conducted one-on-one physical therapy for people who were injured. I could do some training with patients at the direction of a licensed physical therapist, and I had taken a lot of classes in therapeutic massage.

If there was one good thing that came from growing up in River Falls, it was that the Kansas City Chiefs held their annual training camp at UW-RF every year. When I had at last sobered up enough to consider what I could do for money, there had been a really interesting story in the newspaper about the team, trainers, doctors, physical therapists, and the rest of the entourage charged with keeping those million-dollar bodies at the peak of health. It had been like a bolt of lightning. *I could do that.* Maybe not for million-dollar bodies, but for someone who might need a little help. *Someone who might need me.*

I'd met a little resistance from counselors who worried that my past would hold me back or the issues on my record would preclude me from getting licenses. Some people thought I was just trying to get next to hot guys. I guess I had to give them credit for making a deduction based on history. No one could see that I was different from the man I'd been simply by looking at me. I didn't hold it against them.

My new friends and I sat in a circle on the floor while I went over their files. One of my girls, as I thought of them now, emerged almost at once as a de facto leader of the Red Hat tribe. Her name was Sally, and she had smooth silver hair that looked like someone cut it using a bowl. She seemed outspoken, and she was a nudger, elbowing her girlfriends ruthlessly to make her point. Fortunately, no one seemed to mind this treatment. It took a minute for her to settle them down. The whole thing made me feel like I was a counselor back at science camp.

"Izzie was great, and she gave us these wonderful routines," Sally told me, looking around at her girlfriends as if asking them to back her up. "But I was going to ask her today if I should increase reps or weight." She nudged the woman to her right, the same dark-haired woman who had squeezed my arm earlier.

"*Oh.*" The woman winced. "That's right. We've been doing this for about a month, and it's becoming a little easy.

sure to be extra nice to him; his aura's all grassy green with rosy edges." She hung up the phone.

"Grassy green?" I asked.

Izzie gave me a look exactly like one my mother wears when I've done something stupid that pulls on her heartstrings. It was both nice and disconcerting, coming from someone who could easily bench-press my body weight. "Yeah, grassy green. That's a good color, Jordan. It's the color of healing."

"I see," I said, although at the time I didn't put much faith in it. If it made Izzie like me enough to hire me and if it got me special service wherever she was sending me to pick up lunch, it was okay by me.

* * *

Already I could feel the atmosphere of St. Nacho's as it surrounded me, lulling me into what I thought of as a dangerous complacency. People seemed really nice here. Nicer than people really are on the whole. I could already feel it swirling around me, sucking me into a slower pace than even the one I'd known in River Falls. I planned on reserving judgment until later, though. Izzie and I hadn't even gotten around yet to discussing money. I had to make a living, and I didn't know if it would be possible here.

I had to figure out a way to move out of the motel soon, because even though it was dirt cheap as motels go, it was still too expensive for me to stay there indefinitely. I knew that eventually, I'd have to make my presence known to Cooper and Shawn and face whatever they had to say to me when they knew I'd moved into town for good. I knew that I'd need to prove myself to all the people here, and that it still might not be enough to mitigate my past. But first, I knew that if I didn't get Izzie's chicken soft noodle? She was going to be really hungry, and somehow, even as nice as she seemed, I just didn't want to take that chance.

# Chapter Four

I left Day-Use at about five in the evening. Izzie had been telling me to go home for a while, and I would have, except I didn't really have anyplace to go that was nicer than the gym itself, and I was used to working long hours. We'd agreed, with no more than a brief discussion, on a base salary for helping out in the gym and a percentage from massage performed on members there. She said she'd give me a list of the chiropractors and orthopedic doctors in the area. I thought it wouldn't hurt to look in on any active retirement communities as well. If I chose, she told me, I was free to take the portable massage table when the gym wasn't open and use it if I made arrangements for outside clients in their own homes.

It was hard not to look that particular gift horse in the mouth, because it had been my experience that everyone wanted a piece of whatever they could get, even in the nicest places I'd worked. Izzie seemed to just shrug this off. She was an odd sort of woman, and I started worrying about whether she was too good to be true as she almost shooed me out the door with the instruction to "walk around and get to know the place." Since I'd walked there from the motel, I did just that.

I hoped I didn't betray the way my body reacted to those words.

"Mark is a little dramatic," Ken told me, putting out a metal crutch to move us both aside so a woman with a cart could move past. "Lately he's been feeling very put upon because when I came home he had to go back to sharing a room with our brother Kevin."

"How many of you are there?" I asked. I imagined a group of attractive Ashton boys, all lined up like Osmonds, grinning in family photos. As an only child, that sort of thing always seemed so desirable to me.

Mark wrinkled his nose. "Five, two girls and three boys, and everyone has to share but *his highness*, Ken."

"I see." I laughed. "The oldest gets the privilege of sleeping alone?"

"That, and no one can stand him. He wakes up at all hours of the night, screaming and—"

"That's enough," snapped Ken. More gently, he said, "I'm sure no one else needs to hear our problems."

Mark's eyes held genuine regret. "I'm sorry, Ken."

Ken shook his head. "It's fine, Mark." He started past me, and for some reason I couldn't even explain, I didn't want to see him go like that.

"Ken." I stopped him. "I'm staying at the SeaView Motel and it doesn't have a kitchen or anything." I showed him my basket. "Would you and Mark like to get some dinner with me? I'll buy. Maybe you can show me around a little?"

Mark snorted. "If you came here from the SeaView Motel, you've probably already seen everything that's worth looking at."

"Mark," Ken chided. "Mark has practice, and I was going to run him over to the school. We could take a rain check. Or if you want"—he hesitated—"we could get something and eat it there in the bleachers and watch them. His team's pretty good; they're five and oh this season so far." I watched him for a minute after he said it, wondering whether he really meant it or if he was just being polite. A faint flush bloomed on his cheeks and the bridge of his nose. He looked down. "They'll just be running drills; it won't be very exciting."

"Cool. I played soccer," I said. I'd played in school, prison, and with a team from rehab. I wasn't about to elaborate. "I'd like to see that."

"Fine," said Ken, who shifted and turned away. I thought, right then, that he was regretting inviting me and too much of a gentleman to say so. His brother was looking at him with some surprise. Maybe Ken wasn't very social.

I grabbed the rest of the things I needed and met up with the two of them at the checkout. There was only one line, one register, and it had one bored-looking young Latina standing behind it. I noticed that she perked up immediately when she caught sight of Ken, and wondered if he realized it. Izzie had said he was emotionally closed off, so maybe he didn't know the effect he had on others. It might be hard for him to see how attractive he was if he was used to being a superior athlete. Used to a handsome body that functioned like a high-performance race car. It was probably difficult for him to imagine finding love again.

I concentrated on the items in my basket so he wouldn't catch the sadness I was feeling if he looked my way.

Mark interrupted my thoughts. "What's that?" he asked, when I put a jar of Nutella down next to marshmallow fluff on the conveyor.

"Chocolate hazelnut spread," I told him. "It makes the best fluffernutter sandwiches." I realized then that my Midwestern upbringing was showing, even though I'd learned in San Francisco to replace the peanut butter with Nutella. "Well…it's more like a s'mores sandwich."

"No way." Mark looked at me.

I nodded. "Yeah. It's kind of a guilty pleasure. I have good things too." I felt like I ought to defend my choice to buy the sweet treats and the potato bread to put it on by showing that I also had fruit, hummus, whole-wheat pita, and olives. "It makes a great midnight snack." I could feel Ken's eyes on me, but when I looked up, he looked away.

"I'm going to tell my mom to get some," Mark said. His basket was full of things I assumed he was taking to practice, energy drinks, granola bars, oranges.

"Looks like you're the snackmeister for the team today, huh?"

"Mmhmm," Ken said. "Mark never remembers to tell us until we're on our way there."

"Where is practice?" I asked. I hadn't seen a soccer field yet in my wanderings.

"It's up about six blocks past Day-Use. It's real easy to miss it," Ken told me. "Because it's small. The elementary school is right next to the middle school, and behind it is the playing field." Ken pulled out his wallet and paid the cashier.

"And the whole thing backs up to the high school." Mark grimaced. "It's like we go to the same school all our lives."

"If you want, you can come with us if you think you'd have trouble finding the place."

"Yes, that would be good. I'm on foot anyway. I walked to Izzie's from the motel. I was just wandering around before I go back."

We left the small store and walked down the street to where Ken had an SUV parked. We deposited our groceries in the back. The air was cool and crisp. It was still light out and would be for a while, but not as late as it would have been in River Falls. I missed the twilight from the upper Midwest, but since I'd traded it for some pretty spectacular sunsets here in California I didn't feel too cheated.

This close to the coast, though, it seemed a blanket of fog was likely to roll in to obscure the view about half the time. I didn't mind. I liked the way it felt on my skin and the eeriness and allure of a fog-shrouded coastal community spoke to something a little dark in my personality. The day's rain had turned out a perfectly beautiful, crisp early evening, with high, fat clouds that moved quickly inland. Maybe we were due for more rain. It felt like it.

I was looking around when I realized that Ken was holding the passenger door open for me. Mark had gotten into the back without a word.

"I'm sorry," I told him. "I was looking…"

He shrugged and closed the door. When he made his way around, he opened the backseat first and deposited his crutches, then opened the front door, bracing himself on the side of the car as he slid in. He noticed me watching him.

"I'm a motor moron," he said, almost pleasantly, "but you're perfectly safe. I assure you I wouldn't drive if I weren't capable of doing so, and certainly not with my brother in the car."

"I wasn't—"

"It's a perfectly valid question. The mechanics of walking still elude me. I'm relearning a lot of things. But I still have the ability to drive and rather good reaction time."

"That must be a relief," I said.

He shot me a dark look but said nothing.

"Look," I said. "I don't want to put my foot in it every time I say anything. Maybe we should just—"

He sighed. In the mirror on my side of the car, I could see his brother looking out the window as though he found something fascinating there. "No. I'm sorry. You didn't put your foot in it. I'm…I guess I'm overreacting to every little thing." I saw his brother's attention snap back at this.

"It's all right. That's probably natural," I said. "I've worked with people who are coming back from injuries. Some who have had strokes. There doesn't seem to be a single normal way for anyone to behave. I'm sure you're adjusting in your own time. It just takes a lot of it. More than they ever tell you." I said that without thinking. I didn't know what they'd told him, but healing of any kind took a long time.

"I'm sure you're right," he said. He pulled smoothly away from the curb. I had actually been worried that his driving would be less than optimal despite what I'd said. It seemed I had nothing to fear, though, because he maneuvered through the quiet streets of St. Nacho's with ease. We drove through Wendy's for fast food to take with us, not a bad choice, at least not the worst for me. At some fast-food places I would starve. I ordered a side salad, a broccoli-cheese potato, and a Frosty, and when I pulled out my wallet to pay, Ken waved me off. We drove in near silence until we came to Mark's school, and we parked near the field.

Mark trotted—with his bag of snacks—toward the field where his fellow teammates stretched, and I carried dinner while Ken and I made our way to the bottom of the bleachers where we could sit, eat, and watch them run through their drills and scrimmage.

"I take it you went to high school here?" I asked, mostly just to have something to talk about.

He was concentrating on walking over the uneven ground, and he didn't answer right away. "Yes."

I thought maybe the subject was painful for him, so I didn't press. We sat down, and he put his crutches aside. He shook his hands out, opening and closing them, and I fought the urge to help. He pulled out his chicken sandwich and gave me my potato. We each had a salad and Frosty. He looked to where his brother was dribbling his soccer ball through an obstacle course of orange cones and flags.

"It's hard to watch someone you love flail."

"My mom thinks he should move out. Make new friends. It's like he came home to live in his bedroom, looking at the same old Green Day posters, until everything is back to normal. But he'll never be normal again. The only place he goes is to rehab. He should do something."

"It's probably pretty easy to guess what a guy should do in a situation like this if it's not you," I reminded him. "He's grieving. He's healing. It takes a lot longer than you can imagine."

"Do you think he'll get better soon? Izzie does. She badgers him."

"Well, I guess if Izzie's on the case, it must be true; I wouldn't bet against Izzie, ever." I grinned.

Mark grinned back, and we talked about other things, mostly soccer, while he cooled off a little. When Ken came back, he sat down next to me and reached for an orange wedge. "So, did Mark tell you all about me while I was gone?"

Mark blushed, and I said, "We were just comparing soccer coaches. Mine thought I should play a little less aggressively. I probably should have."

"Can I go to Zack's after practice?" Mark asked. "We're going to work on math together."

"You say that, but you'll end up playing with his Wii."

"I promise that's not all we'll do."

Ken shrugged. "I guess that just means I don't have to wait here to take you home." He got a hopeful expression from Mark. "Just remember it's a school night, and you need to be home by ten."

"Zack said his mom would bring me," Mark assured him.

"Fine. Who am I to complain about an evening off chauffeur duty?" Ken started to pick up the trash from our food but realized he needed to pick up his crutches. "Throw this in the trash for me, will you?" Mark took it and loped off to join his friends.

It was hard not to try to help Ken while he was getting his crutches on and finding his feet. I supposed that's part of what was putting his brother on edge. His whole family must be walking around on eggshells, trying to help and not knowing how.

When we were almost back to Ken's car, I decided to say something. "Do you like living at home?"

Ken sort of laughed as he came to a halt and dug his keys out of his pocket. "I knew he was talking about me; he gets this guilty look. I can always tell."

"He's concerned about you and impatient."

"And he doesn't seem to mind sharing my business with the world."

"Sorry," I said, as he unlocked the car remotely and walked to the driver's side. "I've only been here one day and I'm already causing trouble. That's not very surprising, really."

Ken got in with a sigh and shook his head. "Nah. I know my family's concerned." He turned on the ignition. "I don't know what to tell them. I'd like to say healing will take place in exactly fifteen minutes and thirty-five seconds." He turned and backed out of the parking space. As we got going out of the school parking lot, the first fat droplets of rain began hitting the windshield. "I don't know if I'll ever get better."

"You will."

"Why *did* you come to St. Nacho's? You never answered my brother's nosy question."

I considered my answer carefully. "I have friends who live here. I thought I'd get in touch with them. I haven't let them know I'm here yet because I wanted to wait until I was more settled."

"I see."

"Maybe you can help me out. I need to find inexpensive housing. Like a room in somebody's house or a studio apartment, anyplace I can live cheaply. Is there something like that?"

"You could check the grocery store bulletin board. Sometimes people also leave stuff like that on cards on the wall of the Laundromat."

"Yeah, I'm going to need to find one of those too; I don't have a lot of clothes."

It wasn't long before we pulled up into the parking lot of the SeaView Motel. I don't suppose anyone knew why it was called that. You couldn't begin to see the ocean from there.

Before he stopped the car, before I could even begin to gather myself and touch the door handle, he turned to me and said, "Do you have to go? It's early still. Maybe we could get a beer or—"

"I don't drink." I probably gave that a little more emphasis than it deserved.

"Sorry, that was thoughtless." He hesitated. "I don't want you to go."

"Why?" It was my turn to stare. I could see his Adam's apple bob.

"There were other reasons I liked having your hands on me." He looked nervous and younger than he really was.

Suddenly, I wanted two things: I wanted to put my hand on his to reassure him, and I wanted out of that car as fast as I could get. "Well, Izzie will set up massages, and I'll be there for you whenever—"

He shook his head and grabbed for my hand with both of his. "Why is that when you touch me I feel so...?"

"Whoa!" I said. "Whoa, whoa, whoa."

"No, listen to me. I tried to talk to Izzie, but she wouldn't answer my questions."

"Oh, hey!" I was trying to push out of the door, and he was pulling me back.

"You have to listen to me." His voice was on the edge of something I couldn't name, something that spoke to me of late nights, coffee, cigarettes, and people who were there for me when I needed them. People who helped me navigate the more troubling waters of my own life. People I owed a lifetime of gratitude to. "When you touched me, something happened. I felt so *right*. I've been living on the edge of angry and afraid for a long time, and when you touched me it was like..."

I didn't know what game he was playing. People with girlfriends aren't usually my type. *I'm not usually their type.* I didn't know what he wanted, and I was afraid to find out.

I dried off and put on old sweats to warm up, getting into bed without even turning on the television. As I drifted off, the sky opened up and it rained like it rains back home. I could hear thunder and lightning. I was tired and cold, and I fell asleep between the thin white linens, under the nasty blanket and bedspread, without any trouble at all.

I dreamed that Ken was standing on the playing field where we'd watched his brother play soccer, surrounded by Mark's teammates. All of a sudden, Ken took off, running and playing with them, his feet flying, every bit as subtle and coordinated as his brother's. I dreamed Mark looked at me like a kid watching a magic act and I was the magician. He was laughing and crying at the same time, pumping his fist in the air, before he took off after his brother like a puppy.

I'd never seen such joy, or felt happiness like that in my heart, before that dream.

I woke up crying and got the pillow wet and stained with spit and tears.

# **Chapter Six**

I was at Day-Use in the morning before Izzie even pulled up. She drove a tiny car, smaller even than mine, and seemed to take up the whole thing all by herself. She got out and stood up, and it made me think of clowns.

"You're here early." She unlocked the front door of the gym with a rattle of keys. "I'll get you a key; remind me. Then you can open and close if I'm not here."

I thought it was interesting that she'd trust me, an ex-con, with keys. A lot of people wouldn't. Even if I'd never stolen a thing in my life, and my prison stay hadn't been for theft, lots of people didn't think I was trustworthy enough to wash their cars.

"Thank you."

"Thank *you*," she said. "It'll be good to take a morning off here and there." She walked to the switches and started turning on the lights. "You can begin with the men's locker room, and I'll touch up the women's." She wandered off, and we both worked in silence until the first members started coming in. Izzie made a point of introducing me to clients as they came in, reassuring each one that I was competent to answer their questions. She'd adopted me quickly, I thought, almost ruthlessly, as her chief of staff and spokesperson. I actually hoped she knew what she was doing, because I wasn't nearly as certain as she was that I'd fit in.

At one point, a group of three men came in. All of them were bearlike. They had dark, bristly hair and big, stocky bodies. They didn't look related, but looked alike. They each had a thick mustache. Izzie came over, and one of them gave her a hard squeeze, his hands just a little south of what I'd consider a friendly hug.

"Jordan." She called me over. "These are three of St. Nacho's finest. Officer Jim Lundgren, Officer Anthony Brios, and Officer Andrew Callahan. Jordan came in yesterday and I hired him on the spot."

They looked me over as only cops can. I felt like they could read my rap sheet, like it was hanging in the air over my head in a thought balloon. I held out my hand to shake. The squeezer, Andrew, was the first to take it. "Nice to meet you, Jordan."

"Andrew," I said, giving his hand what I thought was a manly sort of pump.

"Andy," Izzie corrected, putting an arm around him and giving him a peck on the cheek. The others shook my hand and were polite but distant.

"Jordan is a massage therapist and he specializes in therapeutic massage. I think you all ought to give him a try. Work out some of that tight-ass cop tension." She grinned at them cheekily while I waited for her to be struck by lightning. I never, ever would have talked to one of River Falls's officers like that. Not even Bill Leviton, who had married Cooper's sister, and considered me part of his extended family.

"I have *you* for that," Andy told her, and I finally figured out that there was more to their situation than met the casual eye. I watched them banter for a minute while I pretended to be looking over a leg press machine. They were...adorable. Izzie, who normally moved like a force of nature, went all soft and feminine around Andy, and even though she still looked like nothing so much as a big drag queen, it suited her.

Andy was letting her spot him while he did presses, and he smiled up at her like she was a goddess. Which, really, looking at her, I guess she was. She wore her unnaturally tinted blonde hair in a halo around her head. Her skin was so tanned it was as if she were the negative of a photograph. She had a lovely face and knew how to enhance it using makeup that was shiny and bronzed-looking. I couldn't fault Andy at all. She was a hell of a woman. And she obviously made him feel like one hell of a man.

I was sort of watching and shaking my head when Brios came up behind me. "She's something, isn't she?" he remarked.

"Yes." I didn't want to talk about my boss behind her back. "Do you work with free weights or the machines?"

"I like the free weights," he said. "But I'm going to run on the treadmill for a while first today." I expected him to move off, but he didn't. I was trying to think of something else to say, but he stopped me.

"Mind if I have a word?" He jerked his head toward the treadmills, and I followed him with a sinking heart. It's not like I don't have a healthy respect for law enforcement and a genuine desire to see the police as a force for good, but I had been a big shit-heel growing up and I had done so many stupid, stupid things. I expected the worst. I expected that he'd run the plates of my car while it was sitting out in the motel parking lot and he was going to tell me I had to leave town.

When we got to the other side of the gym where the treadmills were all lined up facing a television set tuned to CNN, he cleared his throat. *Oh boy, here it comes.*

He looked both ways and licked his lips nervously. "I'd like to get a massage," he admitted. Like it was something clandestine.

"What?"

"I get massages sometimes with the wife; I like it. I like to take a sauna afterward, and my muscles always feel less tight the next day. I find it very refreshing." He looked at me as though daring me to say something. I nodded, silently urging him to go on.

"The thing is, the guys… They like to rib me about it."

I leaned forward. "You want it to be a secret?"

"Yeah," he sighed, and I thought I saw his whole bearlike body relax. I tried not to crack a smile.

"That's fine. How do you want to do this to keep it a secret?"

"Could I come in sometime at night maybe? Not when I'm here with them?" He nodded toward Andy and Jim.

"Sure," I said. "How about you come in tonight whenever it's convenient? I'll be here."

"Seven?"

"Fine, I'll see you then. Can I help you with anything else?" I asked. We'd caught Jim's eye, and Anthony cleared his throat.

"No, thank you," he said in what I guessed was his Officer Anthony voice. "That's fine." I lowered my eyes and went back to free weights to make myself available to spot Jim, if he needed it.

"Son?" Jim asked as I walked past. "Can I talk to you?"

"Yes." I still felt that sense of dread. He jerked his head so I'd follow him. We stood at the side of the room where Izzie kept the free weights in racks.

Jim came right to the point. "I want to get a massage, but I don't want the guys to know about it."

I hid a smile. "I'm here in the evenings."

"I work the night shift. What if I came back by myself in the afternoon? Maybe...four?"

"That's fine," I told him. "But aren't you worried that someone will see you and talk?"

"We could make it look like I was here for something else. I just don't want those two giving me a hard time."

"It's very private. I'd use the therapy room, or—" I wondered if the therapy room would be in use. Maybe Ken would be in there. Clearly, I hadn't given a lot of thought to the details. "Can I get back to you?" I asked him. "There are some things I haven't worked out with Izzie yet."

"Sure, she has my cell number; just call."

"Fine," I told him. I was going to talk to Izzie anyway, but she preempted me by motioning me over to the front where no one could hear us.

"Andy wants a massage, but he's too shy to ask. He wants to know if you'll do it sometime when his friends won't be here."

I laughed out loud.

\* \* \*

By lunchtime, Izzie and I had worked out a schedule of sorts, printing out a daily appointment list where we could each put our names in blocks of time to use the therapy room. I noticed that Izzie placed my name after hers every time Ken was due to come in. I sat at the front counter, frowning down at the paper, wondering how to tell her that maybe it wasn't such a good idea for me to work with Ken when the very man in question set my jar of olives down on the worktop in front of me.

"Hi," I said, putting the paper down.

"Hi." He waited for a minute, and then we both spoke at once.

"Ken—"

"Look, Jordan—"

I nodded to indicate that he should go first.

"Maybe…I thought I should apologize for last night."

"It's fine, Ken. I enjoyed meeting your brother," I told him. That was true, anyway. The dream was still stuck in my head, Mark's joy at having his brother back, my pride at having helped, the happiness at seeing Ken well and happy.

"Then I went and left in a huff." He looked down. "That wasn't right."

"That kind of emotional meltdown doesn't just come and go like a headache, Ken. It still reverberates through your body for a while. You might find that you're sensitive for some time."

"A headache."

"Pardon me?"

Ken was staring at his own hand on the counter, and then he smiled. I could get used to that smile. He had even, white teeth and a dimple that made an appearance on one side of his full lips. His whole face smiled, his eyes crinkled at the corners, and I swear even his ears moved a little in the webs of dark hair that half hid them from view.

"It just struck me funny when you said 'headache.' That's the mother of all understatements. I'm fucking falling apart."

"I know," I told him. I fought the urge to put my hand on his, and when I looked up, his eyes met mine.

"Have you eaten lunch?" he asked.

"I think maybe that's not such a good—"

"Don't think," he snapped. "It's only food." He stared at me for a minute as if I'd let him down in some unfathomably painful way and then turned and began the walk to the front door. Escape seemed to be his backup plan. *Shit.*

"All right," I said impulsively. "If Izzie doesn't need me." He turned back and nodded, waiting.

I went to Izzie's office and asked if there was any reason I shouldn't go to lunch. Half of me wanted her to tell me yes, but she looked at me and smiled vaguely and told me to *go right on ahead.* When I turned to leave, I had an eerie prickling sensation in the back of my neck and thought again that Izzie was kind of disturbing, even though I'd really begun to like her a lot.

I grabbed my jacket from the cupboard under the front desk and followed Ken out into the chilly air. He unlocked his SUV, and I got in. I was putting on my seat belt when he turned and spoke to me. "I'm glad you came. I wasn't sure you would after last night."

I didn't know what to say. I still didn't know what last night was all about. Maybe I'd misread him. Maybe he was just confused and angry. It's not like I'd blame him. He'd been through a lot, and I was just part of the whole lousy package.

"Mark liked you." He started the engine, taking off at a crawl.

"I like him," I said honestly. He pulled out onto the street, and it wasn't long before we were parked in front of an Indian restaurant called Tandoor. He stopped the car and took out his keys.

"I called first; they have vegan dishes on the menu. Are you a vegan or a vegetarian? How strict are you?"

I smiled, absurdly pleased that he'd cared enough to ask. "Not a vegan, no; just no flesh."

Ken shuddered delicately. "When you put it that way, I don't want it either anymore. This place has a buffet, and half of it is vegetable dishes."

We left the car and entered the restaurant. The host motioned for us to sit in one of the red booths along the wall. There were several tables open, and we picked one. The air was redolent with East Indian spices, and it made me feel warm in a way that had nothing to do with food. We sat, both of us glancing between the white tablecloths and the televisions with their Bollywood fantasy musical numbers until a waiter came over and told us to head for the buffet.

I followed Ken. I hated to admit that I'd never eaten Indian food outside of the curried hot dishes that my mom made for church suppers. I'd never exactly been in an Indian restaurant, and the first thing that struck me was the color of all the food. Bright oranges and deep, earthy greens. Yellow cauliflower and potato chunks with bright green peas.

"The colors are pretty," I told him. "But some of it looks…"

"Like baby poop?" Ken laughed.

I snorted. "Kind of."

"Try a little bit of each thing. I don't think you'll be disappointed. Unless you don't like spicy food?" He was concerned for me; I could see it in his eyes. I didn't tell him that before I moved to California I'd hardly ever eaten anything spicier than black pepper, unless Cooper was cooking.

"Wisconsin isn't the land of culinary adventure," I pointed out. "I eat a lot of cheese."

"There's cheese." He showed me. "It's called paneer. It's in this spinach dish, see the white chunks?"

"All right." I filled my plate with blobs of unknown things. I loved the way the food smelled, and when we got back to the table, there was a basket of some sort of flat bread, all blackened and crackled at the edges. I took a piece;

it was hot and glistening with garlic-flavored oil. "This really—"

"I brought you here because I wanted to talk to you about something," he told me, and from the way he said it, my muscles tensed. With my fork halfway to my mouth, dripping with spinach and cheese and rice, I paused, meeting his eyes.

"What?" I didn't know whether I should put the fork down or whether I should eat the food, so I let it sort of hang, dangling there.

He squeezed his napkin in the palm of one hand, his food, it seemed, temporarily forgotten. "I couldn't sleep at all last night. I couldn't stop thinking. It was right there in front of me and I didn't even realize it."

I put my food down and my hands on my own napkin, which was in my lap. Ken's eyes had a kind of tired, edgy glow, and I could tell he hadn't passed a good night. He looked young and kind of breathless. Maybe even fevered.

"I know you'll think this is crazy, but it's perfect, I've already done it. I know we only just met yesterday…but…I want you to move in with me."

"You *what?*" Conversation stopped at the tables next to ours. I lowered my voice. "*What did you say?*"

"I said…" He leaned over, and in an almost theatrical whisper, he hissed, "I want you to move in with me. I rented a house. Well, it's going to need some fixing. It has two bedrooms, two bathrooms. I'll need a roommate, and I'll take the master bedroom with the en suite bath and pay two-thirds of the rent. You can—"

"Wait, you already rented it?"

"Yes, I saw it this morning. I signed the lease just before I came to pick you up." He looked rather pleased with himself. "It's perfect. You need affordable housing, don't you?"

"Well…" I slumped backward against the red vinyl. "Yes, but you don't even know me—I don't even know you! I could be a serial killer. You could be…"

"I could be anyone. Even someone whose name you got off the Laundromat bulletin board, right?" He had a point. "It's not like you'd know them any better than you know me."

I picked up my fork again and toyed with the spinach on my plate before tasting a bite of it. "You're right, of course."

"So why not move in with me? You seem like a polite guy. I tidy up after myself. My family's dying to get rid of me." He broke off a bit of bread and shoved some vegetables on it, then ate them together.

"I'm sure that's not true." I did the same thing, finding the bread delicious with a lentil dish that packed quite a spice wallop. I grabbed for my water.

"Spicy." He grinned at me, and it hit me why I'd be an idiot to move in with him. Yeah, I could find heaven or hell picking an anonymous name off a bulletin board at the market or the Laundromat, but if I moved in with Ken, I had no doubt I'd find both. Heaven because I liked him. He was handsome and funny and he needed me. Hell because he was handsome and funny and I'd need him right back, and wasn't that *just* what I wanted to avoid, now and always? I didn't want personal attachments. I didn't want anything that would take my life out of balance.

He was looking at me anxiously. "So? What do you think? We could go over after lunch and take a look."

I hit on what I thought was the perfect answer. "What happens when I want to bring a man home? I'm not known for my discretion."

That shut him up. For a minute. Then he tilted his head and gave me a sort of challenging grin that maybe scared me more than anything he'd said so far. "If you want to bring a man home? Then do it." He took a long swallow of his water, during which I couldn't help but stare at the long column of his throat again. "Maybe I will too."

# Chapter Seven

"And just what *the hell* do you mean by that?" I asked, and to my shame I saw a blob of food fly from my mouth onto the tablecloth. I dropped my napkin over it quickly and dabbed it away.

"That was classy." He chuckled, and I felt my face burn. "I meant just what I said. If I want to bring a man home, I will. And I just might."

I calmed myself down. I was sure he was speaking figuratively. He was still grieving for his girlfriend, his Amy, and maybe he didn't want involvement any more than I did.

"It's not unusual for someone who has lost a loved one to feel guilty at the thought of ever loving anyone new. They might get confused or have impulses that aren't really based on..." What the hell did I think I was doing? "When the time is right to bring another woman in your life, you'll be—
"

Ken leaned over. "You sure can't take a hint worth a damn, Jordan. If me kissing you didn't make the wheels turn in your head, I don't know what will. I don't *want* another woman. If you've listened to nothing else I've told you, listen to this. Amy and I went out lots of places together, but it wasn't because we were dating. She and I were close. She was my best friend. I loved her, but I wasn't in love with her. I hate that she died when she could have been out safe with some guy who really appreciated her. Who loved her like I never would have in a million years." There was a catch in his voice, and he didn't bother hiding it. "She deserved better than that."

I had no idea what to say to him. None. Except now I had the very best reason in the world not to move in with him if I was smart enough to turn him down. Which, I told myself, I would be. Definitely. Smart enough to *turn him down.*

I left my food untouched after that, and he finished it off. He seemed to be in a better frame of mind, and since I didn't know him, I wondered if he was prone to mood swings.

"So, will you come and look at the place with me? I have the key. It's a dump. I'm going to have to do a lot of work. In fact, I'm wondering how I'll manage it all by myself." He gazed at me. "It's so hard for me to get around these days."

"You have got to be fucking kidding me," I said. "You're playing the guilt card? Who *are* you?"

The waiter brought over the check, and Ken snatched it up. When I started to take out my wallet, he waved me off. "I've got this."

"Ken, have any of your doctors ever talked to you about emotional ups and downs?"

He laughed out loud. "I guess you have a right to ask about my sanity. Before you came along, I was marking time, waiting to get better, feeling sorry for myself that I couldn't live my life the way I'd planned."

"Ken, I've only been here one day, you can't—"

"I went home last night so angry and ashamed."

I'd known he was upset and that I was partly to blame because I'd been incapable of talking to him about it.

"I started thinking about what I want. Little things like being able enter a room without hearing the conversation come to a dead stop. I don't want to worry that my kid brothers will catch me jerking off, or heaven forbid, my sisters. I want to invite someone over and not have six pairs of anxious eyes watching everything I do. I don't want six people to come running when I fall."

"I'll come running," I said. "You know I will. I won't be able to stop myself, and then what will you do?"

"You? I'll tell *you* you're not my mother so fuck off."

"I see. You could hardly say that to the genuine article."

The waiter brought Ken's change, and he took care of the tip and got his crutches ready. He stayed seated for a moment, though, and looked at me thoughtfully. "Maybe it's an emotional high brought on by my meltdown, I don't know. But I suddenly saw a way out of the role of family invalid. The unspoken but very visible way my family slinks around furtively trying to make everything easy for me is making me crazy, and until you said you needed a place to live, I didn't even consider moving out. I didn't want to do it on my own. I was scared."

"Ken." His quiet admission worked toward convincing me, even against my better judgment.

"Just go with me and take a look. It's not going to be a picnic. When I said it was a dump, I wasn't kidding. But along with a lot of hard work comes cheap rent for you and for me, the option to buy the place, which I'm seriously considering. Ninety-five percent convinced. I want this. I'll advertise for a roommate if I have to, but I only looked into it at all in the first place because of you."

"So it doesn't depend on me?"

"No. Neither it, nor I, depend on you." I exhaled the breath I was holding, until he spoke again. "I just want it to be you."

"All right," I said stupidly. "I'll look at it. There are about a million reasons why I should tell you to forget it, and only one to go with you."

"I only need one." He got up. "What is it? If I can ask, that is."

"For some reason I really can't explain, I find I like it a lot when you're happy." I followed him to the door, and when we got out to the parking lot, he turned to me awkwardly on his crutches, grinning.

"In that case, you are so screwed, you should pardon the expression." He unlocked his car remotely and opened the door behind his to put up his crutches. "Because for some reason I can't explain either, *you* make me happy." We both got into the car and said nothing further as he made his way through the streets of Santo Ignacio.

* * *

We passed the high school and headed farther away from the main center of town, until at last he turned on a small side road and pulled up to a tiny, dilapidated house with an unkempt yard. There were several rusted appliances in front of a rickety-looking porch and weeds that grew as high as my thighs.

"Given that you used the word *dump* in your description, I'm not shocked at this point."

"Wait till you see the inside. You will be," he warned, as he gripped his crutches and started up the broken cement walkway to the house.

I couldn't stop myself, and soon I was pushing ahead of him, looking over the porch steps for weak spots. "Watch your step here, it doesn't look very—"

"Shut up, you're not my mother." He caught up and passed me, grinning. "See how easy that's going to be?"

"For you, maybe."

"I checked the porch out earlier. It needs work, but so does everything. I talked to the realtor, and he thinks I should just buy the place. He's pretty sure he'll get the owners to agree to an immediate move-in, and that they'll knock the price down considerably. The market sucks, and this house has been for sale for almost a year. The owners inherited the place and are only renting it to get some cash to pay the property taxes."

I looked around, saying nothing. He got out a key, still on the tag from the realtor's office, and unlocked the door. When it opened, it was both better and worse than I thought. The place was full of junk. Things were stashed in boxes and left littering the ground. There were cobwebs everywhere, and it would need new flooring, paint, and window coverings, not to mention a thousand little repairs. From where I stood, I could see that the kitchen windows were both broken, so heaven only knew what kind of animals had made their home here. On the other hand, on the positive side, it didn't smell like anything had died. *Recently.*

"You are out of your mind," I told him.

"It's a project." He turned to me, his blue eyes serious. "I *need* a project. One that isn't me."

"When you go back to school, you'll have to find tenants. Do you want to be an absentee landlord?" I walked farther into the house, down the hall, and toward the bedrooms. The first bedroom was tiny but had a nice large window that looked out on the front of the house. There was a full bath after that with orange- and cream-colored linoleum. I suspected asbestos.

"I'm not going back to school," Ken said, coming up behind me as I looked at the dirty mirror.

"What?" I tugged on his shoulder to stop him so he'd talk to me. "You have to finish. What kind of job can you get without—"

"I did finish. I was in my last semester when we had the accident. Since then, I've finished all my projects and completed the courses. I graduated with my class in June, but... Well, they cut me some slack, and it's all on the record and official now."

"So you're going to stay in St. Nacho's and work? What are you going to do?"

"I don't know. Teach probably. I'll have to get a teaching certificate. In the meantime, I could just get a job. My parents still want to support me, but..." He shifted around, and I followed him to the master bedroom. Lavender, with big cabbage-flower wallpaper on the walls fairly assaulted us when we entered.

"Have mercy," I sighed. "This goes great with the used appliance lawn art."

Ken barked a laugh and oh, *shit*, how I liked the sound of it. I was so glad to be the guy who made it happen. "You'll love the living room; it has a sweet fireplace. The kitchen isn't big enough to hold a spaghetti pot."

"Can you afford to buy a house?" I asked. "Think about if you don't have a roommate, or if one stiffs you." He raised his eyebrows at me. "For the *rent*."

"Ah. Well, I have money from the insurance settlement, and that will make my monthly mortgage just about...nothing." His eyes lit up for a minute. "Did I mention this house is going dirt cheap? There's still the cost of fixing it up. I'll play the invalid card and get lots of small-town compassion in the form of free labor."

Little by little, his enthusiasm persuaded me. There was no reason that he shouldn't buy himself a house if he wanted one. No reason he shouldn't want to fix it up and live there or rent it or sell it or burn it down. We walked to the living room together, and something scuttled across the floor. Lots of somethings. Burning the place down started looking like a really good idea. I tried hard to keep myself from reacting, but my skin was crawling so I shuddered.

"Yeah, it's...lived-in."

"I wonder if it's haunted too. That'd be like hitting the real estate trifecta, wouldn't it? It's falling down around your ears, it's infested with...crawling things...and when you least expect it, the walls will drip blood."

He watched my face intently. "You *like* it!" he said after a second or so, looking triumphant. "You like it and you're covering it up with disdain."

"How could you tell?" I turned away. I was still trying for disdain, but if the truth were to be told, I actually almost cracked a smile. "The place is completely hopeless."

"So am I," he said softly, coming up so quietly behind me that I wasn't even aware of it until I felt his breath on my neck. His solid presence at my back sparked a host of erotic images in my mind that made my breathing quicken. Yeah. *Yes.* If he'd put his arms around me and pushed me to the ground I'd have gone willingly. When he spoke again, I got goose bumps along my arms. "But I think you like me too."

*I froze.* "That probably isn't a good thing."

"It is for the house," he pointed out. "It is for me."

I stepped away on the pretext of studying the fireplace closely, leaning over and tugging at the vent in the flue to see if it worked. Things I didn't want to even think about fell onto my arm, feathers and great balls of fur and dust, and I jumped back in dismay, knocking Ken off his feet. We both landed on the hard floor, and I hope it was my imagination that I heard a kind of crisp, sickening exoskeleton crunch sound under my ass.

"If I don't get out of here right this second I'm going to start screaming," I said.

"Is that a no?" I stood and pulled him to his feet. He caught his balance with what I suspected was a manufactured excuse to touch me, grabbing my shoulders and pulling me flush against him. For a minute I was too stunned to react; by the time I got my bearings, his hard cock was as obvious as mine. I hung there, caught between two impulses, grinding against him, all the while eyeing the open front door as my only means of escape. When he lowered his head to kiss me, I thought of a thousand reasons why I wasn't good enough for him and broke contact, leaving him puzzled, I guess, in the middle of the living room alone.

Once I was back in the fresh air, I took a deep breath. I wasn't going to mention what happened if he didn't, but I wasn't going to be able to stop thinking about it either. He maneuvered down the porch steps carefully, and not for the first time I wanted to call the irony police and turn myself in. Ken was hot. He burned me up with those blue eyes of his and then played in the ashes. *I was totally fucked.*

"Ken, I think moving in with you is the worst idea I've ever heard for a lot of different reasons. And that house is a total nightmare."

"So the answer is no?" I hated the way he didn't look me in the eye. I wanted him to trust me. I wanted him to laugh again. I wanted to answer all his questions, both spoken and implicit, with a resounding *yes*.

"I want to think about this. It's still a long way from even being yours. You need to think carefully about it as well. I can't promise I'll move in here with you. I can't promise that in the long run you'll want me to. But *if* you get this house, *if* you move in, and *if* you ask me to, you have my word that I'll work as hard as I can, as often as I can, to help you make it habitable."

"What?" I asked her.

"What, what?" She was still staring.

"You're staring at me." I crossed my arms. "Are you trying to freak me out? 'Cause it's working."

"Of course not," she said, humming a little. "I was just enjoying your aura."

"Right, my aura." I still wasn't ready to admit that I believed in such things.

"You are currently emanating a rich cerulean blue with spikes of vibrant pink. Just so you know."

"And what does that mean?" I asked, neatly caught by curiosity in general and a certain tendency to believe the worst, specifically.

"I don't know. It's a color combination I often associate with people falling in love. And oddly enough"—she looked back at her computer and grinned like a stupid person—"I saw it just today on someone else... What was his name again? Oh yeah. Ken Ashton."

# Chapter Eight

I had the first of my clandestine cop massages at four. Jim Lundgren turned out to be a really nice, really stressed-out human being who groaned a little as I worked on muscles that felt as hard as petrified wood. We didn't talk at all, which was just fine with me, and I put him to sleep at one point in the foot massage, so I continued to work, eventually waking him up as I dug around in the large muscles on his back. After an hour, he got up looking fuzzy-headed and ready for another long nap. I made him drink a whole bottle of water, and he tipped me really well.

As I watched him go, I wondered if he would see me differently if he knew about my past. I felt antsy, uneasy in my skin. I could never understand why, especially on days like this when I felt almost happy, I wanted to turn my back on everything and move on. It made me see how my friend Cooper, who for years felt the same guilt over the accident we shared that I did, could spend almost four years never staying in any one place longer than three or four days. Cooper worked through his guilt eventually because he came to realize, as I did, that the responsibility was mine, that he only shared the awful memories.

Cooper is still my best friend, someone who never turned his back on me, even when I deserved it, even when I tried to shift the blame to him. Now I was afraid to call him, to tell him I was in town.

When I thought about Nacho's Bar where he worked in the kitchen, it was with such a wave of longing to see his face it almost made me sick. I had two more appointments and I'd be getting out at about eight thirty. If Izzie didn't have anything planned, I'd walk back to the hotel and take my car down to the beach and tell Cooper I was here.

I hoped he might be glad to see me. I tried to tell myself that it certainly wasn't because Cooper was the only man I'd ever really loved. That suddenly, inexplicably, I wanted to hear his voice.

I told myself it wasn't because someone else was making me think about love.

I snapped myself out of it. Izzie was the one talking about love, wasn't she? Not me. I just wanted to help. It would do me good to remind myself that feeling more than compassion for someone in the midst of their pain could be confusing and disorienting. It was the infamous thirteenth step in a twelve-step program, the reason behind quickie marriages, quicker divorces, Liza and David, and Larry and Liz.

Most importantly, it was the reason for the trail of broken hearts and broken promises that leave people who are physically and emotionally at their lowest ebb even further down on themselves than they were to begin with. I'd attended at least four weddings with the theme "You Raise Me Up," after which people threw each other down with such abandon I feared for their lives. I had avoided this by not allowing myself to get involved with anyone except for work, but now that I was here in St. Nacho's, I thought it might be time to try out, if not love, then the kind of deep friendship I imagined I could form with Cooper and Shawn. The kind I was trying to show Ken.

But isn't it always the way that you make a plan and something happens to blow it all to hell? Ken Ashton, bigger than life and twice as fucking hot, waited for me outside of Day-Use when I left that evening.

Under her breath, I heard Izzie mutter, "Well, I wonder why he's here," when she saw him sitting in his car with the dome lights on, reading the paper. I gave her a look that said I was on to her.

"It's not smart, Izzie. You know better than to shift his focus to me. He needs to heal and feel whole and find someone his own age from a position of strength, not a position of—"

"I haven't seen that boy interested in anything but you since he got out of the hospital. As far as I'm concerned, if it gets him out from under his grandmother's quilts? It's fine with me."

"And when his parents find out he thinks he's in love with his ex-convict masseur and child murderer? What will you tell the police after they kill me when the coroner comes to pick up my body? That you threw him at me? That you hoped he'd fall for someone so completely inadequate that—"

"That's enough out of you," she snapped. "Getting pissy won't make your aura pretty. I don't know why some people

"I have friends who work there. They don't know I'm in town yet." I told myself I should have just kept on going, should have let him think the worst. But when I saw the flare of interest light up his eyes again, it ignited something reckless inside me as well.

"Good friends?" he asked. I found myself doing that leaning thing again. For fuck's sake, I wasn't twelve years old.

"Do you want to come with me?" I asked. "I was going to get my car; you could save me a walk."

He hesitated.

"You're not out," I guessed.

"I never had reason to be."

"Look, I'd rather you didn't go then. It wouldn't be right. Just because I'm going. I don't care what people think about me. You have family to think about." I wanted to protect him. Ken inspired so many emotions I'd never felt before, it was overwhelming.

"It's not just because of you. I haven't lived here for four years. When I came home I moved back in with my folks. I wasn't well. There was no point in rocking the boat. But if I live here, buy a place, then there's no point in hiding who I am either."

"I'm scared for you," I told him honestly. "Too much is changing for you too fast. I think you'll regret it. Go home and rest. Get strong. Buy your house. Put coming out away for the time being. Maybe I'm selfish. I know this whole town is going to blame it on my influence. Once they start looking closely at me, they're going find other things out and then there will be nothing but trouble."

"Are you scared for me or scared for you?" he asked me quietly.

When I didn't answer, he used his key remote to unlock the passenger door.

"Someday, I'm going to walk around and open that door for you." He turned away and got inside. Before he closed the door, he smiled. "But not today."

I walked around and let myself in. I leaned over and caught the seat belt automatically, pulling the straps out and looking for the slot when Ken reached out both hands and cupped my face, bringing me in for a kiss.

What started out tender and tentative almost immediately turned into something else entirely. Even before I thought about it, I'd dropped the belt and put my hands in his dark hair. I'd wanted to do that since I'd first seen him come into the gym. I *had* done that in the guise of massage. His hair was soft and thick and curled rebelliously around my fingers.

Ken made a sound that rumbled through both our bodies as he deepened the kiss. He broke it off and rested his forehead against mine, speaking in a low murmur. "I wanted to get that out of the way...so stupid...always seems so awkward...first-date kiss." He bumped my face with his and moved so that our cheeks were touching. His was smooth, and I smelled a hint of citrus, like he'd just shaved.

"You've kissed me before." I caught my breath. "And that one wasn't awkward."

"Well, yes." He smiled against my skin. "And no. I just wanted to do it again."

I brushed my lips back over his and pulled away a little. Ken sighed and started up the car. We drove through town again in silence. I could have asked him about the house, whether he'd made any decisions. For that matter, he could have asked me if I'd given any thought to moving in with him yet. I don't know why he didn't, but I admired him for it. He took my hand about halfway to Nacho's and simply brushed his thumb over the back of it. It soothed and aroused at the same time. When Nacho's came into view, he parked some little way down the street. I got out of the car first and came around while he reached over the seat and fished in the back for his crutches. He opened the door and stood, slipping his hands into the arm brackets and gripping the handles.

"The doctor says it won't be long before I can ditch these and go to two canes," he told me, walking along beside me. "Thanks to Izzie's torture."

"Yeah? That's great. I'll bet you'll be glad to get rid of those."

"Not nearly as glad as I was to get rid of the walker."

I laughed. "Not exactly a *GQ* top-ten accessory. My clients always hate using a walker, young or old." As we neared the bar, I could hear music. There were a number of people on the sidewalk, standing around smoking. Some were holding beer. I hadn't consciously given that much thought, that everywhere I'd look tonight someone would be drinking. It was for damned sure not going to be me. Ken broke into my thoughts.

"I started in a wheelchair. So…progress." I looked at his feet, imagining how hard it would be if my body didn't do what I told it to do.

"Izzie told me your prognosis is good, that you have every reason to assume you'll recover almost completely."

"Yep." He grunted, negotiating around the people who loitered near Nacho's entrance. "I'll even play the violin again."

"Really?" I thought of Cooper. "I didn't know you played the violin."

"I don't. It was a joke." He looked at me. "You know the one?"

"Yeah." I was distracted at that moment by the music I was hearing, a Mexican mariachi tune played on a violin. It could only be Cooper playing.

"What is it?" Ken turned back when he realized I'd stopped walking alongside him.

I don't know why hearing Cooper play like that caught me so unprepared. I knew Cooper entertained the patrons of Nacho's with his violin before the management pushed the tables back and the DJ turned on the dance music. He'd told me. But when I heard Cooper again—something so impossibly familiar to me—memories caught my heart in a vise that physically hurt until my throat practically closed. I had to stand still for minute while shock traveled through my body. I hadn't realized, hadn't understood how much I'd missed Cooper until right then.

The last time I had seen Cooper, he'd visited me at Hazelden in Minnesota when I went for my second stab at rehab. He'd held me and we'd cried, and then I had him thrown out and taken off my list of approved visitors. At the time, he understood. I wanted him to move on, to go back to California with Shawn and to cut his ties to a past that could only drown him in remorse.

Yet suddenly I worried that maybe he'd seen that differently. Maybe he thought I didn't want his friendship anymore. That maybe I was cutting ties forever.

So now, faced with the prospect of telling him I'd come to St. Nacho's and that I really cherished his and Shawn's friendship and needed it, I thought maybe I'd gone about building up to it rather badly.

Ken turned to face me, concerned. "What?"

"I don't know if I can do this. My friend and I, we left it a little…open-ended."

Ken's face went blank. Like a mask. "Open-ended how?"

"Like maybe he won't want to see me open-ended."

"There's only one way to find out."

"And if he's unhappy I moved here?"

"Is he the mayor?"

I laughed. "No."

"Then he probably can't have you kicked out of town." Ken grinned and then sobered. "You didn't move here to get back with him?"

"No." I was quick to reassure him of that. "He has someone, and they're happy. It's good." I bit my lip. *Didn't that sound like I wanted to get back together, but he was taken?* "It's not like that between us anyway."

"Was it ever?" Ken asked.

"Yes."

"I see." He had that blank look again, the one I didn't know how to deal with. He was too young, I thought, to hide his emotions well. Maybe he was just too new at feeling his way with his attraction to men.

"If I promise to tell you the entire story sometime, you have to promise to learn to hide your emotions better. Everything you think shows up on your face."

He shrugged. "Fair enough." He took my hand again, pulling me back against a building as a small group of men walked past. "I just want you to know I don't think I've ever cared what happens to my face before. You're probably the first person who has ever made me feel this off balance." He looked down at his legs. "So to speak."

"Ken, have you ever been with a man before?"

He kept his eyes down, and even in the spotty illumination of the streetlights, I could see that his cheeks were burning. "Yes. Well...groping. Furtive exchanges, mostly related to sports. Locker-room stuff."

"You've never had a lover?" I asked, point-blank.

"No."

"Oh, for fuck's sake." I wanted to go home. Not just to the motel, but back to Wisconsin. "You don't make things easy, do you?"

He backed me up against the concrete wall of the building next to Nacho's and pressed his hand into my groin, lighting it on fire as though he touched a match to a fuse.

slowly, making allowances for Ken. He took us right up to Cooper, inside Nacho's Bar, as though he were a bird dog bringing a kill back to its master. He presented us, beaming, and both spoke and signed, "Look what I found."

Cooper's playing faltered, something I'd rarely, if ever, seen, and next thing I knew, he shoved his instrument into Shawn's large hands and threw his arms around me, clutching at me hard, nearly cutting off my air supply. I could hear him breathe in, and I wondered, because I was trying to do the same, if I smelled as much like home to him as he did to me.

"Damn, Jordie," he whispered in my ear. "Missed you."

"Me too," I told him. We broke apart, and I knew I wasn't the only one feeling a little overwhelmed by my emotions. "This is my friend Ken."

"Hi." Cooper held out his hand, and Ken shook it, his crutch dangling from his forearm as he did so. "I've seen you around here, haven't I?"

"Maybe. I've lived here all my life. Except when I went away to school."

"Are you back home for good now?" Cooper asked him.

Shawn looked on; I didn't know how much he was getting of the conversation, but I'd noticed when we'd first met that he always seemed to enjoy simply looking at Cooper.

"Yeah, well. I think so." Ken looked at me. "Maybe not entirely for *good.*"

I felt the blood heat my face, and Cooper looked amused. "I'm going to play another couple of songs, and then it's going to get too loud here to talk. Let's go to Shawn's and my place, where we can all catch up." He signed something to Shawn, and Shawn nodded and signed something back.

Cooper took his instrument back from Shawn and began to play, this time a lighthearted Irish fiddle tune, and something happy bubbled up inside me. Shawn came up beside me and asked me if I wanted iced tea and I nodded, and he said something to Ken then, who nodded as well. Soon he took off, and Ken and I were left alone. Ken pushed me toward an empty table on the patio, where we could still hear Cooper play. The air was moist with fog and smelled like the ocean. I was going to love that about living in Santo Ignacio. Everywhere you went, everything smelled like the sea. It even got onto your clothes and hair, and you felt it through your skin to your bones.

Shawn came by with three iced teas, and he had no sooner placed them on our table than he went and got me an ashtray.

I pushed the ashtray away and shook my head. "I quit," I said. Shawn raised his eyebrows. He had such an expressive face that I couldn't help but watch and wait for the next thing to skitter over it.

"Good for you," he told me sincerely.

"You smoked?" Ken asked.

I nodded. "Yeah. I was completely and unrepentantly polluted back in the day."

"Yeah?"

"Yeah." I felt his eyes on me, so I studied my tea, using my straw to push a piece of lemon around. "Now I'm so clean, I squeak."

"Do you?" He grinned. I felt my cheeks heat. I couldn't decide if I liked this new, flirtatious Ken. "I would like to test that out."

I tried not to laugh, but it got the best of me.

Shawn looked from one of us to the other. "How long have you been in town?" he asked.

I held up two fingers. "Two days."

Shawn didn't react to that. "It's good to see you. You look healthy."

I nodded. We sat sipping our tea and listened to Cooper play. Ken remarked more than once that Cooper was amazing. I had to agree. He'd gotten better since the last time I'd heard him practice in the apartment we'd shared in River Falls. We fought that day—all my fault, as usual—and I pulled a stunt I wasn't proud of and ended up first in the hospital and then back in rehab. Not because I'd used, which always made people I knew from Hazelden laugh. But I'd lied to myself and everyone around me and found a number of creative ways to self-destruct with behavior that was toxic and counterproductive—continued to "act out" as my counselor put it—and pretty much hurt everyone who ever cared about me.

Seeing old friends was good, unless you had been a total shit-heel when you'd seen them last. I had that embarrassed feeling I get when people talk about old times, and I realized Shawn was probably aware of every mistake I had ever made.

Shawn reached over then and placed his hand on mine. I met his eyes and found nothing but friendship and compassion.

My face threatened to crumple a little, but I hid it by taking a sip of tea. I heard Cooper finish a piece with a tremendously complicated ending, adding that dash of arrogance—the result of being a child prodigy. Ken's eyes met mine.

Cooper came in moments later with the violin case I recognized as the same battered one he'd always carried. We had probably been about eleven when he'd received his first full-size violin. Since then, he'd changed instruments twice, I think, but he still used the same battered rectangular case, modified at one point to be strapped to his back when he rode his bike. It was covered in the scraped-up remains of rock-band stickers. He saw me smiling at it.

"Time flies," he said, hugging me hard. "Follow us home, and we can catch up a little." He looked up at Ken. "If it's okay with your friend."

Ken seemed curious. His face was pleasant but otherwise unreadable. We finished our tea and walked to the boardwalk with Cooper and Shawn, who held hands. I knew they slowed down for Ken's sake. I was conscious of him beside me and admitted to myself that I would have liked to hold his hand or put my arm around him, but his crutches made that not only difficult but also maybe even a little dangerous.

We reached a little side street between Nacho's and the pier and turned away from the beach toward the entrance of a small apartment building with a courtyard on the ground floor, and eight apartments that I could see, four up and four down, surrounding it. We went up some cracked cement stairs to one of the doors, painted red with 2C in gold letters screwed onto it.

"This is ours," Cooper said. He watched as Shawn took out a key and unlocked the door, flipping lights on as we entered. It was a tiny apartment, light and beachy. It had a soft sofa with a muted tropical print and wicker tables and side chairs. Cooper must have caught the look on my face, because he laughed. "It came furnished."

Shawn took off his jacket and hung it in the closet. I removed mine. Ken wasn't wearing one, and I wondered if he just found it too complicated putting a jacket on and taking it off, although with all those muscles he probably didn't suffer in the cold.

"So," said Cooper, motioning me to the sofa. "Can I get you anything to drink?"

I looked at Ken, and he shook his head. "Nothing for us, thanks," I told him. I felt awkward now, away from the chaos of the bar. "You go ahead, though."

"I'll grab some waters," Cooper said, signing to Shawn. I couldn't get over how self-assured his signing had become. When I'd seen him last, he was just beginning to learn. At the time I'd discouraged it. I'd been peevish and jealous. Now it shamed me.

When they had their waters, they sat in one chair, Cooper on Shawn's lap. It looked so natural I thought maybe they sat that way a lot. "So, how long are you in town for?"

I hoped my answer wouldn't be an unpleasant surprise. "I...indefinitely. I plan to live here," I told them. Cooper signed this for Shawn, and thank fuck he smiled as though he was genuinely pleased. "I got a job at the gym. Day-Use Ex Machina." I flushed. No matter how many times I said that, I felt like an idiot.

"Izzie's place?" Cooper asked. I nodded. "Small world. What do you do there?"

I told him I did therapeutic massage and personal training. Even to my own ears it sounded dumb, and I think he had trouble signing it for Shawn. "I got my bachelor's degree," I told him. "Then I came to San Francisco and got a massage therapy license and a personal training certification. I got a job as an assistant to physical therapists. I've spent a year or so doing massage for people with sports injuries. I help keep their muscles resilient, put them through their paces. It's actually kind of cool. My clients included a couple of players from the Oakland A's."

"Yeah?" Cooper asked. "Real baseball players?"

"Yeah." I noticed Ken flinch. "I'm helping Izzie out in the gym, and I'm taking massage clients. She gave me the numbers of local doctors, and if I don't find enough business here in town, I'll check into surrounding towns. I'll make time for you anytime, though."

"That sounds great," Shawn said, after reading Cooper's signed translation. He gave Cooper a gentle poke in the ribs. "That's what you can get me for Christmas."

"I can also bring the table here," I said. Cooper was looking at me, and I couldn't read him. I wondered if after everything we'd been through he'd believe I had changed. Whether he could ever trust me again. I wondered if he was thinking of all the times I'd messed up, of all the times I'd let him down.

I was sitting in his living room talking about a new life and a different career, an actual career this time, not just a job, and I wondered if he was waiting for the first sign that I was going to let everything go to hell again. Out of the corner of my eye, I saw Ken roll his shoulders, and without even thinking about it, I pushed him a little to get him onto the floor between my legs where I could work on his muscles.

Cooper was watching, and Shawn smiled. "Have you found someplace to live yet?" Shawn asked.

Ken spoke up. "Jordan will be moving in with me."

I frowned a little. "I haven't said yes." I pushed my thumb along the sternocleidomastoid muscles on both sides of his neck, ironing out his tension. Walking with crutches really did a number on the human body.

He groaned a little and smiled. "Did I mention how cheap rent could be if you did this all the time?"

I gave him a little extra thumb when he said that. "I pay my own way."

He winced, reached up, and brought my mouth down on his. When I managed to break his hold on me, he looked completely innocent. I glanced up to find both Shawn and Cooper looking at us with unreadable faces.

"What?"

"You're such a turd. You should have called." Cooper signed something to Shawn, who nodded. "I had no idea you were in the Bay Area. We'd have come to see you."

"I'm here now," I told them, although I was looking down at Ken as I used my elbow on the place where his shoulder met his neck. I couldn't tell whether he was falling asleep or passing out from the pain. "Are you okay?"

"Fuck yeah," Ken said, and even though he said it, he didn't look like he was okay at all. His eyes were closing, and I thought he might be dozing off.

"Since my ride is falling asleep here, I think it's time for us to leave."

"All right. You know where to find us." He and Shawn rose from the chair. "We can reach you at the gym, right?"

"Yep, I'm there. But I'm staying at the SeaView Motel." I watched Ken right himself without helping, which I knew he might resent in front of Shawn and Cooper.

Ken said, "For now." I ignored him.

"I do couples massage." I knew if Cooper told Shawn that, I'd be seeing him sooner rather than later. Cooper gripped me in a strong hug. I returned it, once again feeling the history between us. Cooper was home for me. More than my own family, more than the town we grew up in. Cooper was home for me, and always would be. He gave me one of his rare, genuine smiles, and I hugged Shawn and left.

As we walked back along the boardwalk, Ken seemed pensive. "You love him," he finally said.

"Yes. I love him." It was the honest truth. "He saved my life. I'll never be able to repay him enough—"

"You *love* him," Ken said again, and I let out the breath I was holding.

"Ken, I know I love him. I've admitted I love him." I stopped him from walking away, so he would look at me while I was talking to him. "In order to tell you about it, I'll have to explain everything, and I don't want to go into that now. I'm tired and hungry. Aren't you hungry?"

"Now that you mention it." He nodded. "We could get something. Takeout, maybe. Go to your place."

"You never give up, do you?"

He grinned at me and bit his lip. "A positive attitude is all part of being a winner." When he said it, he affected an accent that made it sound like "weener."

"What?" I wondered if I'd heard correctly.

"When I was a kid one of my Little League coaches was from the Dominican Republic. I used to love when he gave a pep talk. 'Everybody wants to be a weener. When you are a weener, you can write your own teecket.' After a while, I realized he did some of it, the weener part, on purpose because our whining made him crazy."

I looked at my watch and found it was ten o'clock. "What's open to eat around here this late?"

"Ah." Ken gave me a mysterious smile. "If you ask anybody in town, they'll tell you, if you don't want fast food, there's only one place to eat in St. Nacho's after ten."

"And that is?"

"A closely guarded secret, unless you're inviting me home." He waited.

I contemplated him for a minute. His blue eyes glittered in the light of the Nacho's sign, and he gave me that slow, lazy smile that could stop my heart. I saw the way the muscles of his arms bunched as he put his weight on his crutches. I had firsthand knowledge of exactly how those muscles would feel beneath my hands. Hell yes, I was inviting him in. What the fuck? Did I have *stupid* written on my forehead?

Well, shit. *Right.* I probably did.

# Chapter Ten

I wrapped my hands around what was—arguably—the best mu shu vegetable, pancake-wrapped Chinese burrito I'd ever had, getting comfortable, and sat cross-legged on my motel room bed when it hit me. I'd probably never been this relaxed, this comfortable, with anyone except Cooper, ever.

"So, what do you think?" Ken used the small wooden, snap-apart chopsticks to dig into St. Nacho's very own Yen Chin "Three Ingredients Taste." "Was it worth taking a chance I might violate your airspace?"

"Would you do this with your physical therapist?" I asked.

"No, but she's a big Romanian girl with a mustache like Stalin. You're not my physical therapist. You're my masseur. Why don't you come here and lay your hands on me?" He shot me a cheeky grin.

I rubbed the hand that wasn't holding my burrito over my face, which was a mistake because I got plum sauce in my eye. "Ow, shit!" I grabbed a napkin and started scrubbing at it. I felt Ken's big, gentle hand take hold of my wrist.

"Stop, you'll make it worse," he said. "Let it tear up a minute and then dab." He held the napkin with such delicacy. He touched it to the corner of my eye, and I began to feel better immediately. I was blinking frantically, but when I could focus, his face came into view inches away from mine. He dropped the trash into the bag between us.

"You still have some sauce," he murmured, cupping the back of my head and bringing me in for what I thought would be a kiss. I closed my eyes and was shocked to feel his tongue lap at my cheek. "Mm. Good."

He was so close his breath misted my face, the pungent garlic aroma not unpleasant when the scent of Chinese food was all around us. "What are you afraid of?" he asked.

"I don't want to see you get hurt. I don't want to feel like I'm overstepping—"

"Come on. You work ridiculously long hours from what I've seen. Did you do that when you were in the Bay Area too?"

I nodded. "Yeah. I guess."

"Well, then where did you meet guys?"

I was silent for a while. I didn't really want to have to tell him I didn't meet guys. I didn't want to get into a discussion of just how long it had been since I'd been with someone, because I sensed that was just the sort of leverage he was looking for. "Here and there."

"In the Laundromat? In the garden department at Home Depot?"

I looked away, but I could feel him watching me. I noticed his chopsticks were in his left hand. I decided to change the subject. "Are you a lefty?"

"Yes." He allowed the conversation to drift. I watched him put a perfectly juicy-looking shrimp in his mouth. He smiled around it for a minute and then began to chew. There was a little sauce on his lips, making them glisten when he smiled at me. "If you keep looking at me like that, we're not even going to finish dinner."

"Fine." I took a deep breath. "Let's see. Big, left-handed... First baseman, am I right?"

"How come not pitcher?"

I dared a hand on his beefy shoulder, letting it trail down his back over his traps and his lats. "You need all this for batting, not pitching."

He nodded. "You play?"

"Sure, in school. But my true sport was competitive chaos, and my hometown was so small we didn't even have enough players to field a team."

"You're pretty hard on yourself."

"I earned it. Look, Ken," I told him, putting my food down. "When I was young, I thought I was bulletproof. I was such a jerk. I hardly ever got caught. Cooper and I were smart enough, and in his case talented enough, that we could talk our way out of all kinds of crap we should have caught hell for."

"And?" He put his food down too, and I could tell he was bracing himself for the honesty I promised him, but it scared me. I'd told the story often enough. I'd even gone with the MADD groups in Wisconsin and the Bay Area to talk to kids in school. If there was anything I could do to keep one more person from fucking up like I had, I was determined to do it. But it was hard, here in this hotel room with someone I admitted, if only to myself, that I cared about.

"I was at a graduation party for some friends who were a couple of years behind me in school. No... Well, they weren't friends. I guess I can say that now. We just crashed every party we knew about in those days." I lowered my eyes. "Where there'd be booze. I wanted to leave; it was boring, and the afternoon had been long and hot. It was a huge party, and there were people everywhere. I was agitated for some reason; I don't even remember why. I was such a shit. I didn't want to stay at a dull party when there might be another with more going on. Cooper said he was too drunk to drive. He told me he thought we should take a nap in one of the bedrooms, sleep it off. It was twilight, so it was around nine, maybe nine thirty. It gets dark late in River Falls in June.

"I don't know why I was so insistent, that's the thing. I try to remember back, but it's a blur now. Cooper gave me his keys and said flat out he wasn't driving drunk. I took them and told him to get in the damned truck. We were still fighting when I started backing out of the driveway." I swallowed hard. "What we didn't know, *what neither of us could possibly have known*, was that Bobby Johnson, the little brother of the girl who was throwing the party, was out there on his Big Wheel. He was so low to the ground, I never saw him. I heard the plastic scrape—"

"Oh *shit*." Ken put his head in his hands.

"The rest is distorted in my memory." I placed what was left of my food back into the foil wrappers it came in and put it away. No way was I eating anything else. "I went to jail. That was before the truth in sentencing laws went into effect, and I was still eligible for early release. I don't know what would have become of me if—"

Ken wrapped his arms around me. He held me in a hard embrace, as if lending me his strength. "Shh."

"I can't," I told him. "You don't understand. I'm not like you, not like everyone else. I owe something I can never repay. I can't be distracted. I can't forget. I can't let it all go and just be…pleasured. Not anymore."

"At the risk of sounding flip, you could just pleasure me."

"Oh, fuck you!" I wanted to push him off the bed, but at the last second I remembered how hard it would be for him to get up.

"If you insist."

It was either kill him or lean back against the headboard in defeat. My head hit the cheap laminate really hard and sent it crashing against the wall. "Are you *trying* to be an insensitive jerk?"

"Will it make you look at my lips again?"

I turned away with what I hoped was contempt. Probably from his point of view, it looked more like longing. Maybe I *was* conflicted.

He stroked the skin of my arm with a finger. "I get that you think you have to pay for your past. I'm the last person who would want you to forget what you did."

"So what's all this then?" I asked. "I'm the first gay man who's come along?"

"In St. Nacho's? Hardly." Ken laughed. "Maybe the first since the accident."

"Great." I got up and went to the bathroom to get the plastic bucket for ice. "You want a soda or anything?"

"Coke would be nice." He turned where he was sitting on the bed as I picked up my key. "You know how attracted I am to you, right? You know that when you come back through that door, I'm going to do everything I can to make something happen between us."

*Jeez.* I stopped before opening the door. "Yes." I didn't want to turn around and see him lying on the bed, watching me with those blue eyes. I swallowed hard and pulled open the door. "Coke?"

"Please," he answered.

On my way to the ice machine, I couldn't think about anything but how it felt when Ken pulled me into his body. The rush of that embrace was so enticing I'd have walked over broken glass to feel it. There was heat there, and I'd been cold for a long time. It's not like I didn't want things to be different. I wanted to be pure and shiny and new for Ken, the way he was for me. Not used and filled with guilt. I wanted to offer him something he couldn't get in a thousand other places, but I didn't have anything to offer except the almost painful desire I had inside of me to see him happy.

It didn't stop me from bringing back sodas and ice with the single-minded determination to be the best thing he would experience between the sheets in his life, ever. The best first time. The most conscientious lover. It didn't stop me from imagining his cock sliding between my lips or my ass cheeks. It didn't stop me from entering the room, setting the sodas down next to the ice bucket, and crawling up between his legs on the bed to show him how I kiss a man when I'm serious. I took his face in both my hands, and for the briefest flicker of a moment I could tell he had last-minute doubts.

"Too late," I told him, bringing his mouth to mine in a way that left not a single question about who had the experience between us.

"Good," he hummed against my lips.

My throat closed around a barely whispered, "Say yes."

"*Yes.*" He sighed against me in surrender, gripping my shoulders as he opened for me.

I broke the kiss to travel down his throat, tasting his skin as I went. His hands moved across the muscles of my back, mapping out my shoulder blades, the ridges in my spine. I felt his callused palms slip down the back of my jeans to circle my ass cheeks a little, and then he squeezed them and pulled me up and into him at the same time, fitting our bodies together.

"I love your muscles," I told him, unbuttoning his shirt and slipping my hand inside. "Love this skin." He had crisp dark hair I'd seen before when I'd worked on him. Now I let my fingers play, finding the swirls of hair that surrounded his sensitive nipples. He hissed out a breath when I ran a fingernail lightly across one of the buds, pink and rippling under my touch. I used my other hand to spread the fabric apart so I could reach it with my mouth.

"Oh. *Sweet,*" he said when I teased his nipple with my tongue. He dug his fingers into my hair and held me to him. I slipped a hand lower.

"What's off-limits?" I asked. "Anything hurt?"

"Nothing," he replied between panting breaths. "Nothing is off-limits. Just keep going—" His head fell back when I cupped his package with my hand. I flicked open the button on his jeans, feeling around before opening the zipper. His underwear was already damp with precum.

"Maybe instead of limits I should have asked what you hope will happen." I was working my way down a trail of hair that led to the curly thatch I was uncovering. I slipped his jeans and briefs off his hips, pushing them down his long, strong legs and off when it occurred to me how hard it must be for him to look at his body, which for all intents and purposes was strong and whole, and know that it didn't work.

When he didn't answer right away, I looked up at him and saw the stain of arousal on his cheeks and across his chest.

"Everything," he told me finally, pulling his arms out of the sleeves of his shirt and tossing it on the floor by the bed. "Whatever you want."

My cheeks burned. I wanted to taste him. I wanted to suck his dick and fuck him with my tongue. I didn't say it out loud. I just worked my way lower and lower until he couldn't mistake my intentions. I reached an arm up to pull my toiletry kit off the nightstand, opening it with a spill of razors and shaving cream and Band-Aids until I found condoms and lube.

"Latex okay?" I asked. I hated it. Hated the taste, even the flavored ones, but I never made a move without them. That didn't mean I didn't give his cock an experimental lick up the underside, along the vein, just to taste his skin and feel his pulse beat there.

"Yeah," he said. "Whatever, yeah." I remembered being that new. The "whatever, yeah" stage, and I was determined to protect him, from me, from disappointment, from disease. From *whatever.*

I rolled the condom down his cock with my mouth, mostly because I could and I wanted to show off. I slipped my arms under his thighs and pressed my face against his balls. He was gorgeous. Big and sweaty, and all mine for a little time at least. I sucked first one and then the other testicle into my mouth, playing with them, stretching the skin and letting it pop out with a little tug. I licked the sensitive skin behind his balls down to his hole. When I ran a gentle tongue around the tightly puckered flesh there, he jumped like he'd been hit by lightning. There was no way to describe the effect being in control of Ken's body had on me. I flicked him with my tongue again and blew on the dark skin a little, and he jerked and shivered in my hands. I laid them flat on his abdomen, holding him down so he wouldn't jump and break my nose, and breached his ass with my tongue.

Oh yeah. That got his attention.

"Holy mother of... *Fuck!*"

I wrapped a firm hand around the base of his cock near his balls, and then I murmured against his most sensitive skin, "Buckle up, *Junior.*"

# Chapter Eleven

Ken's legs trembled next to my ears as I moved from his ass to his gorgeous cock. He was thick and long, with a perfect, fat mushroom crown that had a spot just beneath it that made his legs shake uncontrollably when I gave it even the slightest bit of attention. I wrapped my lips around the head, swirling my tongue over the slit in the tip through the latex, and his hips jumped for me again. I could tell he didn't expect it either. He had no idea what his body was going to do from one minute to the next.

I knew what it was not going to do… It was not going to come until I was damned good and ready. Until I had my fill of that velvety-soft sac against my face, until I had pushed my fingers into his tight heat. He wasn't going to have to beg; we were way past begging and halfway to incoherent puddle of goo.

I took him deep, calling on all my arcane, magical dick-sucking powers to catch him off guard, to bring him to the edge and pull him back from it. I don't know why I was so determined to control him like that, except that I could, and maybe I wouldn't get another chance. There were plenty of hot, young guys standing around at Nacho's Bar every night who wouldn't remind him of the worst day of his life every time he looked at them. I was as certain as anything that sooner or later he'd look at me and see just another drunk driver. Or he'd see me as nothing more than a guy who'd sucked him off when he was curious.

Eventually, when he wasn't desperate to get laid, he'd want to look for the right guy, and I was the guy right now. It didn't hurt so much while he was thrashing beneath my hands, fucking my mouth deeper and deeper, taking advantage of the fact that I could take him where he was determined to go.

I found the lube with one hand while I kept up a rhythm on his cock. He was making these noises, tight, strangled little moans that made me want to keep it up forever. I chanced a glance up and saw him, one hand over his eyes, one fisted in the sheet. His jaw was clenched. I wanted to touch him inside, to find his sweet spot first with my fingers, then with my cock. I circled the entrance I'd breached with my tongue with a delicate finger. Whatever I wanted from him, however desperately I wanted it, I had no intention of hurting him. I could take my time. As I slipped past that first tight ring of muscle, his hand moved toward my arm and he looked at me, saying nothing. I pushed farther, slickly pumping my finger in and out a few times while watching him carefully, my mouth still on his cock.

Ken's enthusiasm flagged a little at the invasion, and I redoubled my efforts, hoping to confuse his body with pleasure and pain until they merged and blended and he transcended thought. Until his body took over and gave itself up to me. When his hips shifted and he moved against my hand, I added another finger. It wasn't long before he was consciously surging between my fingers and my mouth, reaching for the orgasm I wasn't allowing him to have. He gave a frustrated groan and then cried out incoherently when I added a third finger.

"Yes." He jerked. "Hard." He snapped his hips at me. "Mmn. More."

"Shh," I told him, after letting his dick go with a *pop*. I pulled my hand away from his cock and then swallowed him down completely, working him with my throat. There was nothing to stop him from coming now, and I felt it rip through him like a storm, the way his body convulsed in my hands, the sudden heat inside the latex. He was muffling his own cries, having snatched a pillow off the bed. I moved up and over him, removing my fingers. I grabbed another condom package and tore it open with my teeth.

"May I?" I asked, taking the spent condom off his cock. I tossed it on the floor next to the bed. His eyes opened wide as he perceived what I wanted. We hung there frozen, eyes locked, breath mingling, still shivering, Ken from the aftermath of orgasm and me from need. I watched his expressive face as he gauged whether he wanted me that way.

"You can trust me to make it good for you," I breathed against his ear. "And you can tell me no and it will be all right." I may have confused the issue a little, though, by sinking against the warmth of his body, because I'd never felt anything like the searing sweetness of his skin against mine.

He drew me to him, giving me tacit permission by sliding his hands down my sides to my hips and opening his legs to cradle me in all that heat. His hole was soft and ready but tight, and *fuck*, it felt so good to be that close to him, skin to skin all along the length of that hard body.

I fought his muscles for a minute, but I was kissing him as he lay beneath me, unquestioning and maybe a little blown away. I whispered for him to breathe for me as distress registered on his face. He fought the invasion as the head of my dick pressed against him intimately, but he bumped and rubbed his face against mine and closed his eyes. Suddenly I was swallowed up in heat and sensation. It felt like finding the safest place in the world to be during an earthquake. His body was still rippling and quivering with every slick slip and slide of mine.

*So responsive.*

Something lit his eyes as they watched me, some kind of surprise maybe, or passion, as his body gave in and melted under mine, as he bloomed and accommodated me. Moved against me. He gave me everything he was made of with those eyes. I swallowed hard and let go, wanting to take him someplace we could only go like this, just once, together, for his first time. I never wanted to be more, or better, for any man. My own orgasm was building within me, had been building since he'd let me take him with my mouth, and I reached an arm down and around his hips to hold him to me.

Suddenly I was flying—soaring—toward my release. When I slid into the bliss of it, I took him with me all the way, feeling his body clench hard and quiver against mine again as though each wave of erotic pleasure was happening to both of us in the same exact way. I couldn't close my eyes, and we shared that as well; he watched me, his eyes going a deep purplish color that I'd only ever seen in the twilight sky back home.

I drove into him one final time and stayed, pressed as deep as I could reach within him, and we melted together like wax. He made these noises, half moaning, half begging, while I filled the latex. Despite his size, I felt absurdly tender with him, almost rocking him, cradling his body in my arms as my heated skin cooled and my dick softened and slipped from him.

He kissed me again. It was as if we couldn't get close enough. I ditched the used condom and tucked my face into the junction of his neck and shoulder and was almost tired enough to fall asleep there.

I don't know when I began to perceive that he was becoming restless.

"What time do you need to be home?" I asked him. It was one, or close to it.

"Probably pretty soon. They worry." He started to push me off. "More than they did before the accident."

"You can use the phone to reassure them." I admit I was all about curling into his warmth and falling asleep.

"I have a phone," he said. He pulled away, and I thought I saw the first sign of regret. "I can't call them and tell them I'm staying out all night. Not yet. Not like this. They have no idea…"

I caught a faint whiff of fear in the way he said that. "Ken," I began.

"Where are my…?" He looked around.

"I'll get them," I told him. I went around and found his clothes. "Here."

"I'll need my crutches too." He didn't look at me. He *wouldn't* look at me.

I went and picked them up from where he'd placed them next to the bed. I didn't say anything either, just handed them over.

"Maybe if you called to let them know you're on your way. Then you won't have to rush—"

"They're probably already asleep," he said, not even realizing that they couldn't be asleep and worrying at the same time. I could see he was panicking.

"Look, don't you think we should—"

"I've been late before, they'll understand, they just… I don't know. They might worry more now. Since I got hurt, they baby me."

"Ken—"

"They don't even know I'm dating."

"You're dating?"

"Smart-ass." He relaxed a minute and smiled again. "I probably should…" He looked at me. "I'm completely losing it."

"I guessed."

"Can I have some time?" he asked. "I'm really going to need some time." He put his hand on the side of my face and rubbed my lower lip with his thumb. "You *look* like you just sucked me off."

I snorted. I couldn't help it. "Dick lips. I know."

"If I… Are you going to be okay?"

"Sure," I lied. "You need time, take it."

"I'll see you tomorrow at the gym. I have an appointment."

"I'll be there," I told him. I would too. And I wouldn't even be wearing that "fucked and fucked over" face I used to get when guys played hit-and-run and I was too young to hide how much it pissed me off. When he was fully dressed, he used his crutches to push himself to his feet.

"Look," he said. "I just need a little time."

I stood next to the bed, watching as each move he made sped up. It was as though he was taxiing down a runway in order to, as the McGee poem says, "Slip the surly bond of earth."

I allowed nothing to betray my emotions as he put his hand to the knob of the motel room door. I could wait until after he left to feel it. His back straightened for a moment, and he twisted, putting his crutch behind him so he could balance. "I guess I'll be seeing you."

I knew then I could have said something to keep him there. If I'd betrayed even a hint of hurt feelings, he probably would have turned around and stayed for a while. But this was his date with reality, and frankly, three would have been a crowd.

"Drive safely," I told him. That was something I could mean with my whole heart, and I'm sure I even fabricated a smile. Like it was the "be the bigger man" Olympics and I was going for the gold.

After he left, I ground my teeth in frustration. It wasn't exactly the end I'd planned to the evening. I watched the news for about an hour and turned the lights out. Sleep was slow in coming. Tomorrow the maids would come in, eliminating all traces of men and sex and Chinese food from the room.

Just another day in St. Nacho's.

# Chapter Twelve

Izzie gave me a little sideways glance when I walked into Day-Use, but said nothing. Given her ability, according to my Red Hat ladies, to know when someone had been "getting some," I kept an eye on her face for clues. Could she tell? Was I reading way too much into local rumor and speculation? I did an extra-careful scrub on the men's locker room to keep some space between us.

The morning wore on, and my Red Hat ladies came in to work out. If I stayed in Santo Ignacio, there would be a rhythm to my days. The cops seemed to come in on Mondays, Wednesdays, and Fridays, except Andy, who stopped by more often. The "girls," as they called themselves, from the Red Hat Society came in on Tuesdays and Thursdays. Ken came in Tuesdays, Thursdays, and Saturdays for personal training, and he was down on my client list, a chunk of time blocked off after his hour with Izzie each time.

I was beginning to feel the heartbeat of the place; I could see the invisible ties that bound all its inhabitants together. I found out there was a good-natured rivalry between the firefighters and the police that often turned into active combat at the Labor Day picnic on the beach and the Fourth of July baseball game, but then was under strict cease-fire during the "Bears for Kids" and "Spark of Love" toy drives at Christmas.

I learned that Izzie volunteered her time at the local schools in a grassroots effort aimed at eradicating childhood obesity in Santo Ignacio, and that anyone who was hungry and couldn't afford to pay would get a takeout meal at Yen Chin with no questions asked.

If I stayed in Santo Ignacio, these people would fold me into the batter that made up their community, asking nothing more of me than to be nice and play by the rules. And from what I could tell, there weren't that many of those. I was never sure, though, that it wouldn't go all to hell when people knew about me, which is why since I had gotten out of rehab the second time I'd generally tried to keep one foot outside of any door.

I heard a voice behind me. "You gonna polish the vinyl off that thing, or can I use it?" *Andy.* Izzie's boyfriend. I'd been using a Clorox wipe on the pad of a weight bench, and I'd apparently been doing it in an idle way for a while.

"Sure," I told him. I looked around for Izzie and didn't find her. "Do you want me to spot you?"

"Yeah, if you think you can." He smirked. "You're a bitty thing compared to my Izzie."

"Yeah, well," I murmured, standing over him as he began his presses. "That applies to everyone around here. She's pretty strong."

"I know. At first I found it kind of disconcerting."

I grinned. I'd dated a gym bunny or two in my day and kind of liked being crushed a little, but not everyone did, especially, I figured, by a woman. "It might take some getting used to."

"It did," he confided. "The first few dates I had to keep reminding myself I was armed."

I snorted. At least he was honest and open to new things. "She's hot, though."

"Oh hell, yeah," he said, doing the last of his eight reps. I helped him put the bar up. He flexed his arms while he waited between sets. "And sweet. When my first wife died, I thought maybe I'd never love anyone again."

"I'm sorry," I murmured automatically.

"It's all right. Time passes."

"You never forget, though, do you?" I said it without thinking, but it made him look at me in that cop way that made the sweat prickle under my arms.

"No. You never do."

I looked at him as he lay there, and I felt an overwhelming urge to confess. "Can I tell you something?" I blurted.

"Mmhmm," he assented, gripping the weight bar in his strong hands again.

"I mean, it's something I want to tell you because I was thinking about making my home here, and it seems like unless I tell I'll never feel right," I nattered on as he counted his reps under his breath. "It's not like you won't find out if you ever have to pull me over or something...so..."

"Eight," he puffed out, and I helped him put the weight bar up again. He gave me his full attention, saying nothing.

"I did some time in Wisconsin behind what they call an OWI felony," I told him. "OWI is operating while intoxicated, it's like a DUI here—"

"I know what it is, son," he said. Could he have been more coplike at the moment? Calling me son like that? All it needed was aviator shades, a rifle, and the words *spread 'em.*

"Anyway, I caused the death of a very young child while under the influence of alcohol. I served time. It's all in my rap sheet. You might as well pass it around. I don't want anyone to make any judgments about me without knowing all the facts."

"Izzie was right; you need a sign," he muttered, gripping the weight bar again.

I froze. "What?"

"Izzie told me you practically tried to talk her out of hiring you." He panted. "Five. You should probably stop leading with your jaw. There isn't a cop around here who doesn't see ordinary people do stupid things every day. There's some really bad people, and then there's some really decent people who make really bad decisions."

I kept my eyes on his but said nothing, holding my hands out for the bar when he was done.

"Eight." He sighed. "Did you do your time?"

"Yes."

"Rehab, making amends?" he asked.

"As much as humanly possible." It wasn't like I could bring the boy back. If I could have, even if it cost me my life,

I would have. But that was pretty easy to say since I wouldn't have to actually do it, and so it fell into the "talk is cheap" category. Sometimes I didn't even trust myself enough to believe it.

"You'll never have a clean slate, Jordan," he told me honestly. "You'll have to answer to your creator. And if you screw up like that again, especially in this town, I won't hesitate to hunt you down and make you pay."

"I understand, sir."

"But if you've made your way back and continue to do what's right? Then I'll be glad to call you my friend." He held out his hand for me to shake, and I almost lost it, until I saw Izzie peeking out from behind the entranceway door and realized she'd set this moment up for me. Was I that predictable?

"Thank you." I cleared my throat. "Thank you, sir."

"Andy," he told me, grabbing his workout towel and heading for the treadmills.

*Andy.* I said the name in my head as he moved away. He reminded me of Bill, back home. Cooper's brother-in-law. He once told me police officers see the worst that life has to offer, but that among the people he could count as his friends, they were often the most determined that things could be better. I felt more relaxed as I slipped back in among my girls.

My Red Hat ladies were all over the news that Ken Ashton was purchasing a house in Santo Ignacio. Apparently news traveled as fast here as it did in any small town. They cheerfully filled me in on the house's former occupants and were already making plans for a grand housewarming party for him. I floated with them from machine to machine as they enveloped me in their aging-lady chatter and made me feel like a well-loved pet.

Sally, my outspoken bowl-haired lady, took me aside. "You know," she said. "We know most of the young ladies here in town, or their mothers. We'd be happy to organize a little something..." She looked at me expectantly.

For some reason, I found this way more difficult than telling Officer Andy I'd killed someone. My gut clenched, and I had a moment of terrible indecision. "I—"

Ann came up from behind. "You're embarrassing the boy."

"I am almost thirty," I pointed out.

"So a little party? To introduce you around?" Sally persisted.

I sighed. "It's probably better that I introduce myself around at Nacho's Bar," I said, waiting for the fallout. "After ten."

"Oh." Sally frowned. "I see."

"I'm sorry," I said, stupidly wishing her frown would go away and we could return to the easy banter we'd been enjoying.

"Why should you be sorry? I'll just plan a different kind of party."

*Oh, jeez.* "Um," I hedged, and for an awful minute I pictured Sally and her bowl cut answering the door with an enormous vat of Crisco and an ice-cream scoop.

"Well." She brightened. "When you find a place, we'll just throw a housewarming party for you too."

"He's moving in with me," a low voice rumbled from behind me. I turned to see Ken slowly working his way to the therapy room. Was it my imagination, or did he look tired and out of sorts?

Sally's eyebrows disappeared right up into her hair.

"I haven't said yes yet," I told her.

"No point in saying no." Ken turned as he opened the door. "Resistance is futile." He slammed the door shut behind him, hard.

A guy doesn't shout "what the fuck?" in a crowd of ladies old enough to be his mother. Not if he was raised by *my* mom, the woman who dragged me to the River Falls Methodist Church every Sunday, spit-sticking my cowlicks down and thumbing the lipstick she got on my face off after kissing me, while I stood there dying of embarrassment by inches. Not if he was a gentleman, anyway, so I held it in.

"What the *fuck* was that?" Sally muttered.

* * *

An hour later, Izzie motioned me back to the therapy room. "He's ready for you, hon," she said as she walked past me. I opened the door and found Ken on the massage table, on his side facing the far wall. This time he seemed to just be wearing his boxers. A stack of fluffy towels lay on a table beside the door, so I picked one up and went to him.

I started by picking up the pump-top container of body lotion. "Did you like the aroma of the lotion I used last time?"

"Yes," he said, still facing away.

"It's got a eucalyptus smell to it." I put a generous amount in the palm of one hand, and I placed my other hand on his shoulder. "If you could just lie on your back?"

He rolled back but threw his arm over his face. "I don't know how you can be so nice to me after what I did last night." He looked over his hand at me. "Unless you were also just being *nice* to me then."

I pulled his arm from his face and began, as I always do, working shoulders and pecs. "You know that's not the case."

"I'm sorry, Jordan. I'm so damned sorry." He caught my hand midstroke on his chest. "I panicked."

"I know that, Ken," I told him. "Relax now. We'll talk later." In minutes I had him heaving a generous sigh. I was relearning his body, lengthening and stretching muscles that were tight from working out and anxiety.

The song playing on Izzie's music system, heard only distantly from this quiet room, was one I remembered from years before, a song that always made me feel a little hopeful, a little restless. It made me think of cold winter nights and finding the warmth of a lover's body between the sheets. I'd once told Cooper that I missed our younger days when we thought we were immortal. I'd used the words "when we were high school fucking gods."

Looking back, I couldn't imagine how I didn't see that for the insanity it was. Here, I was laying my hands on a man who needed me to help him use his body; here, where I had the power to give him relief and pleasure, whatever form that might take; *here*, I was a god.

I leaned over and brushed my lips to his, the barest touch. It wasn't right to do it, not while I was working, but I felt his body relax into the table then, as he shuddered through another sigh.

"I don't know why I panicked."

"Shh," I told him again. "This is your time to just feel. We'll talk, I promise." I wasn't really sure if I wanted to keep that promise. I'd had an endless night, during which I remembered my long-standing rule never to get involved with people who weren't out. Sure, Ken presented a major temptation. His fine ballplayer's body was right there for me to see even if I was trying to forget. But he was a client, and more importantly, in a transitional place in his life. *How could I have ever been so stupid?* As long as I didn't think of him as anything more than a man who was experimenting with me because I represented safety for him, I would be fine.

*Sure I would.*

Like it or not, this time when I was massaging his hands, running my thumbs over the callused pads at the base of each finger, I was imagining licking and sucking each one. When I worked the muscles in his thighs and calves, I was envisioning slipping between them and pulling his legs around my waist. It was a kind of torture, really, as I imagined taking each delicate toe into my mouth.

Despite my less-than-wholesome thoughts, the entire time I worked I took my cue from the spiritual massage set, also envisioning healing, wrapping it around him like a warm white light. He was silent as I worked the large muscles in his back, but once again I felt his body shake with sobs.

"Why is this happening to me?" he asked, in a voice muffled by the arms he'd locked around his head.

"I don't know," I said. "Maybe you need it."

"I can't live like this," he murmured. "I can't be bursting into tears all the time."

"Does it happen all the time? Or just when I'm working your muscles?"

"Just here."

"Think of it as spiritual rust then. Once we grind it off, it'll be gone. Like the Tin Man in *The Wizard of Oz*."

He gave a wet chuckle at that.

When I was finished, I went to get him a bottle of water. He seemed weak; when I brought it in, he was still just lying there.

I handed him the water as he swung his legs over the side of the table. I braced it, still afraid that given his size he was at the limit of what it could hold without wobbling or tipping over. Maybe if business was good enough, I'd be able to put in one of those big heated tables they use in spas.

"Was Izzie tough on you today?"

"In more ways than one," he said. "Izzie's powers of observation are legendary. She asked me why my aura looked fucked and yours looked fucked over."

*Only in St. Nacho's.*

"Oh well, at least you won't have to set her straight. Those Red Hat ladies are innocent-looking enough, but they've already threatened to introduce me to 'nice girls.'"

"What did you tell them?"

"Just before *you* announced I was moving in with you? I told them I would probably do better at Nacho's Bar."

"Well, that's that then."

"What?"

"Trina's the president of the local chapter of PFLAG. I'm out. My mom will hear about this before she leaves the office today." Ken reached for his shirt and began slipping it on, buttoning it while still sitting on the table. He looked ill.

"Which one is Trina again?" I brought his pants to him and found his shoes and socks. I turned the sock balls right-side out.

"Tall, hair cut short in back, fluffy all around her face. Shrewd eyes." He smoothed his shirt down. His keys and wallet fell out of his pants when he went to put them on, and he cursed. I picked them up while he worked at pulling both legs of his pants up, drawing them free of his feet. He then let himself down off the table to pull them up and zip them. Unobtrusively, I still held the table steady. He slipped his arms into his crutches.

"Trina," I said. "I could talk to her. Tell her it's not what she thinks—"

He leaned over and kissed my cheek. "Thanks, but that's not necessary. I'll talk to my family. I...I still need some time, Jordan."

That seemed absurd to me, if only because during the brief two days I'd known him he'd been pursuing me pretty fucking relentlessly. He'd gotten past my defenses, broken down my resistance, let me fuck him, and then fled like a schoolgirl. I thought at the time that regret was a funny thing. I wasn't even sure he understood his desire to get away from me, but I thought I'd make it easy, so he didn't have to gnaw his arm off or anything.

"That's fine," I told him, when what I really wanted to say was, *Are you out of your fucking mind?*

He put a hand to my face, letting his crutch dangle from his forearm like big, ugly jewelry. "Thank you." He thumbed my cheek and pressed his lips to mine, first hitting the corner of my mouth so I thought it was a mistake in aim, but then repeating the gesture symmetrically, one side and then the other, his breath quickening pleasantly against my skin until he reached his target and used his tongue to ask for entry. Whatever I had resolved to do only seconds before, it wasn't long before I was winding both my arms around him and allowing him to lift me to my toes. I was afraid to wrap my entire body around his for fear we'd knock the table over and cause a scene.

That didn't stop me from wanting to get as close as I possibly could to Ken's hard body. In no time he was taking over, doing what came instinctively, grinding against the junction of my thighs and making me a spectacle in my track pants. When we pulled apart it was a near thing, because I couldn't tell which one of us stopped, but we stood there panting, tented, leaking, and very much ready to tear each other's clothing off. Neither one of us said a word, and there was a long damned silence while we waited for our bodies to settle down. Ken took a second bottle of water, this time from his gym bag, and as he drank it, I pictured him swallowing my cum and nearly lost control right then and there.

He left without saying anything. He just shot me an "I'm not through with you" glance and left.

It was for damn sure I'd have liked to know what Izzie had to say about my aura right then.

# Chapter Thirteen

I worked for the rest of the day and then retreated to my hotel room. I'd never given Ken my cell phone number, and I didn't think anyone else would call, so I shut it off and tossed it on the nightstand with my keys and my wallet. I undressed, slid between the sheets, and reached for the television remote, but about then I became aware of how tired I was, how long the hours were that I'd been working, and how difficult the previous days had been for me. I drifted off in no time in the silence and gloom.

When the hotel phone rang at two in the morning, I dragged myself awake. No one I cared about would call me at two a.m. I lifted my arm up enough to flick the plug out of the back of the handset, stopping its clamor. I was groggy but managed to get myself a glass of water before I fell back into bed and dragged a pillow over my head. Sometime later, I awoke to a loud and erratic pounding on the door.

Cursing, I lurched up. I was naked, so I hopped into jeans on the way to answer, nearly losing my balance, and reached out a hand keep myself from falling. My momentum made me hit the door with a hard smack.

"What. The. Fuck," I said when I opened the door to find Ken standing there. He put a hand out as though he thought I'd slam the door in his face, and stuck his head in to look around.

"Are you alone?" he asked. I don't know what pissed me off more: that he thought I might not be or that he had the nerve to ask. He looked terrible. His eyes were red and his cheeks were darkly stubbled and rough.

"Of course I'm alone. Do you have any idea what time it is?"

He turned those red-rimmed eyes on me. "Why didn't you answer the phone, Jordan?"

"I was sleeping... I was tired." *Now* my fucking head hurt too. I turned, giving him room to come in. "A lot has happened in the last three days."

He let out a mirthless laugh. I sat on the bed, and he stood towering over me. Not for the first time I almost shivered, looking at that solid body of his. He was glowering, which made him even *hotter*, and *how sick was that?* I watched his hands clenching and unclenching on the grips of his crutches and I needed to swallow hard. Despite his lack of balance, he began to pace. It intrigued me to watch his body mechanics. They improved remarkably with anger.

"You just don't get it, do you?" he said. He swiped his hand through his hair, the crutch dangling from his forearm dangerously close to whacking him in the face.

"What?" I asked. "Coming out? I sure the hell do get it, junior. I had to do it. And don't kid yourself if you think even ten years has dimmed the memory. My father still chooses not to sit in the same room with me." I felt myself soften a little. "Was it bad?"

"Yes." He sat down with a *thump* and sighed. "No."

"That clarifies things."

"Shut the fuck up." He glared at me. "It was bad because it was so… They hardly batted an eye."

"What?"

"I told my parents, and they were like, 'Thank you for telling us. Anything else?' It was awful."

"Ah." I nodded. "Awful. I always thought that awful looked more like people throwing your clothes out the window. More like spittle flying or shots fired."

"Don't you dare make light of this."

"What do you expect me to say until you tell me what's wrong?" I asked. "It's too fucking late for guessing games." I flopped onto my back, moving up to put my head on the pillow. He could talk, and if he didn't make more sense I would try to fall back to sleep. He dropped into the bed beside me, and I heard his crutches hit the floor.

"They were fine. Amazingly supportive until…"

"Until what?" I never noticed, but the corners of the ceiling were full of cobwebs. It was disconcerting because I didn't see any spiders. I kept thinking if there were cobwebs there had to be spiders, and the fact that I didn't see them made my skin crawl a little. In the meantime, Ken, who had gotten me out of a deep sleep in the middle of the night and apparently *forgotten* what it was that had upset him so much, was lying there next to me saying fucking nothing for the longest time.

"Until I told them about *you*," he said grimly. "Then they lost it completely."

I forgot all about the spiders. I forgot a lot of things that made me vaguely uncomfortable in that moment and focused on the one thing that sort of, even though I had tried to prepare myself for it, broke my heart.

I spoke past the pain. "Sorry."

"Sorry?" he muttered. "Is that all I get? Sorry?"

"Fuck you! What do you want? I've got nothing but sorry." I turned away from him. "Don't let the door hit you."

"Jordan—"

"Get out, Ken," I said. "I'm tired, and tomorrow is going to be another long day."

I felt an arm wrap around me. "I'm not going anywhere. You know I'm not going, but if it makes you feel better, you can tell me to go again."

"I don't know what to do," I told him.

He slipped away and sat up for a moment. I heard fabric rustling behind me. "Let's get some sleep," he said, dragging my jeans off.

"Ken—"

"Shh." He slipped up behind me again, wearing nothing but his underwear, and pulled me back against his chest. "C'mere. We don't have to talk, we don't have to fuck, let's just get some sleep."

"Okay," I told him weakly. I could feel his knit boxers against my cold skin. He was warm everywhere, wrapping himself around me. Whatever drama was surrounding him with his parents, I could still feel that hum of rightness when his skin touched mine. I guessed it was simple chemistry. I couldn't remember another man, another person, who made me feel so good. Even Cooper, who felt like home, didn't feel like this.

Ken spooned up to me, and I reached around and hooked a hand behind his neck, bringing him in for a brief kiss. He seemed as tired as I was.

I asked him, "Anything else that needs to be said tonight?" It might be a good idea to let me know if his dad was going to show up with a gun.

"Nope." He squeezed me hard, which I took to mean *shut up.* I fell asleep with his breath softly disturbing the hair on the nape of my neck.

* * *

I woke up before Ken, feeling his strong arms wrapped around me as the first rays of sunlight began to tease their way through the gap between the inexpensive light-blocking draperies. Motes of dust danced in the beams, and I watched them without moving or saying anything for a while. Gradually, Ken stirred. I felt the first faint changes in the way he was breathing against my skin, a barely perceptible tightening of his hands as they caressed me, and the answering flush in my body as his cock filled and tightened against my ass.

I settled back farther against him, absently wondering if his hard-on was for me or if it was just everyday morning wood. A hand slipped around me and cupped my balls. I got my answer.

"This feels good," he murmured against my hair.

"Yeah?" I hardly dared to breathe. He was pulling me closer and grinding on me, setting sparks all along the trail of kisses he was leaving on my neck with beard-roughened skin.

"Yeah." He backed away briefly, pulling his shorts off and tossing them over the side of the bed. He ran a hand down the column of my spine, moving so slowly that it felt like water dripping, or something teasing along my skin like a bit of fabric, like silk. I didn't know what kind of experience he had, but his touch felt innocent, like an exploration, not a seduction.

I bit my lip to keep from hurrying him along. His hand trailed lower and lower at an impossibly slow rate, until it slipped down my ass crack to tease my hole and gently rub the skin beneath it toward my balls. I opened my legs to give him room, and he laughed against my ear, a kind of delighted chuckle, as though he'd made a discovery and wanted to test his theory out.

"Your skin is so soft here." He tickled me.

"Well…" I gasped when his finger circled around behind my balls and then teased at them. They drew up a little as my dick tightened. "It's not like it gets a lot of wear and tear these days."

"Mm." He pressed against me so his erection found friction against my leg. "I want… What do I want?"

"You have to ask?" I rolled a little to see his face.

He bit his lip and blushed. *Blushed.* "I want to fuck you. Do you? I mean…is it okay?"

# Chapter Fourteen

"Whoa!" I held my hands up in a time-out gesture. "In here." Mark followed me to Izzie's office. I caught her eye as we went in, and it was pretty clear I had tacit permission to use the room. I left the door partially open behind us and indicated that he should sit in the chair. Instead of sitting at Izzie's desk, I leaned against it, facing him. We contemplated each other for a couple of minutes before he got going again.

"Dang," he said. He looked at his feet. "I didn't have you figured for a guy like that."

"What exactly did Ken tell you?" I asked.

"Nothing," Mark said. "He didn't have to. Mom and Dad were shouting, and you could hear them down the street."

I cringed.

"You drift in here and get a job, and three days later my brother's spending the night with you in a motel? That's crazy. He was with Amy forever. He wouldn't just turn around and...switch."

"So what do you think happened?" I could see he was going to have a hard time explaining it away using only my personal charm as a motivating factor.

He tried a different tack. "Ken could have any girl he wants. He just thinks he's damaged goods, and you're letting him think it! If he believed in himself, if you didn't reinforce the whole cripple thing…" He didn't know what to do with his hands. I really liked this kid a lot. I didn't want to be the guy that "turned his brother queer," even if he was happier with that version of the truth than with admitting his brother might have been gay to start with. I didn't want him to look at me with those angry eyes.

"Do you really believe it's like that? That he'd just be with a guy because he doesn't think he could get with girls?"

"Well—"

"Does that even make sense? You're old enough to know what men do with other men. Do you think your brother would—"

"Jeez. Shut up!" Mark covered his ears, and I would have laughed except he was so serious and I didn't want to disrespect him.

"I think you need to ask your brother some honest questions," I said.

"So do I," came a voice from outside the room. I looked up and saw Ken come through the door. "Mom got a call from the school that you ditched. Somehow I had a hunch you might come here."

Mark looked down at his feet again.

"Whatever's between me and Jordan is our private business."

"But—" Mark started.

Ken cut him off. "Since you're my brother and you're concerned for me, I'll answer whatever questions you may have." Ken tilted his head down and gave Mark a kind of forearms into them and turned away. "If you can figure out how I should feel right now, call me," he said without looking back. "Izzie has my number."

\* \* \*

I spent the rest of that day in a fog. I worked hard and had two new clients. They were both long-distance runners, young women who'd been friends since high school and trained for marathons together. I liked working on them, and it seemed like they got something out of it, saying they would definitely be back. They tipped me well and left smiling.

I was going to like living in St. Nacho's, but I could see I'd made a misstep getting involved with Ken. I was drawn to him. I was concerned for him, but I didn't know if I wanted what he offered. I wasn't prepared to have my life in St. Nacho's complicated by a relationship. It had only been three damned days, and already I was caught up in something I didn't completely understand.

To my surprise, around dinnertime Cooper called. He told me Shawn was busy with rehearsals and he thought we could grab dinner if I felt like it. I was happy to have a plan that didn't include eating grapes and a sandwich in my hotel room. He came by on his bike with a spare helmet.

"You still don't drive?" I asked him.

He rolled his eyes. "Looks like my phobia is here to stay. I can't seem to get over it."

I felt such sorrow at that. "My fault," I told him. "I'm so sorry."

"I do all right. I don't need to drive much." He grinned. "I can if I have to, at least."

"Now it's more of a strong preference?" At one time his fear of cars was so powerful he became physically ill.

"Yeah." He grinned. "I don't tell Shawn that or I'd have to give up the Harley."

I put on Cooper's extra helmet. "Can't have that."

"Where to?" he asked me.

I thought about how heavy my heart had been feeling all day. It felt lighter already, now that Coop was here. "Anywhere," I told him. "Everywhere. You decide."

Cooper gave me a wink and put on his own helmet, firing up the Sportster. "Got it," he said. "One anywhere, coming up."

All my good memories of high school came roaring back with the sound of that engine. Starting in the spring of sophomore year, Cooper's fascination with motorcycles in general and the Harley-Davidson in particular had begun. How many nights had I spent lying in my bed listening for the sound of that bike on the highway, far enough away from my home that my parents didn't connect the noise to Cooper, and close enough that when I sneaked out the window I could meet up with him, hardly breaking a sweat, in five minutes? How many hot summer nights had we spent getting up to mischief using a bike just like this one, parking and camping by the Kinnickinnick River, eating fast food and drinking beer filched from one or the other of our parents?

I leaned forward and wrapped my hands around his rib cage now, where once I might have wrapped them around Cooper's waist, maybe inched them down below his belt, jerking him off while he hauled ass down a country road. Now we screamed up the Pacific Coast Highway at a far more civilized pace than we used to and he belonged to someone else. I was... I didn't know what I was, except for grateful that I still had a friend like Cooper.

There wasn't a lot I could count on in the world; there never had been. My old man spent most of his waking hours trying to catch the perfect buzz. He had scared my mom and me when I was growing up, and now, that fear had turned to anger and disgust. My mom was resigned to a life that meant walking around on eggshells every minute of every day. I wasn't.

Cooper was my knight in shining armor in those days, riding up the highway on his Harley. All these years later, I still saw in him the kind of quiet stillness that spoke of true strength, not the bluster and chaos of my father's brutality. I wonder now if I would have stood even the slimmest chance at a decent life without his example.

*Probably not.*

Even through jail, even afterward when I was lost and still lying to myself and everyone around me, I had Cooper to show me how a real man could live his life. I wanted to mold myself and cling to him from behind as we rode along, but I didn't out of respect for Shawn.

When at last we stopped at a mom-and-pop Mexican place in some beach town almost an hour and a half up the coast from St. Nacho's, Cooper dragged the helmet off his sweaty head. Ruffling up his short hair, he led me into the restaurant. We sat in a booth and tucked our helmets on the seats beside us.

The place was mostly a dive by anyone's standards, but Cooper had a gift for sourcing great out-of-the-way places to eat. I had no doubt he'd tell me what to order as well.

The booths were red vinyl piped with yellow, and the floor was a dingy sort of white linoleum. There were tables and chairs set in the middle of the room, but they seemed to have nothing in common with the booths, as they were wooden and nondescript, as dismal as the booths were cheery.

A glass wall on one side looked out on the ocean, past yet another set of tables that matched neither of the two I'd already seen. These round cement tables, surrounded by semicircular benches embedded with pebbles, were topped with multicolored umbrellas. Now the umbrellas were cranked down and the view was spectacular. Fires dotted the beach where people were using fire rings. The water itself seemed as smooth and tranquil as Cooper; the whole of it soothed my spirit like nothing else had for years.

The paper menu looked like it had been handwritten in the twenties. Cooper shot me a look when the waiter came over that I recognized as his "do you trust me?" look. I had enjoyed more than one excellent meal in the wake of that look.

I gestured for him to order for us. "Knock yourself out." I grinned. "Except I'm a vegetarian."

"For real?"

I nodded.

Cooper gave the waiter instructions for a plate of grilled fish tacos topped with cabbage for himself and a grilled vegetable plate with queso fresco and tortillas for me, no beans or rice unless they were meat-free.

"So," Cooper began, drumming his fingers on the table. "You think you're going to like living in St. Nacho's?"

"Yeah," I said. "I don't think three days is much to go on, but it feels good there, like I'm someplace I could call home."

Cooper watched me with an unreadable look. "Shawn was concerned that you would find it a little quiet."

"Yeah. Well." I had some apologies to make to Shawn, and if I lived to be a hundred, I'd probably only scratch the surface. "I'm not the same man I was, Coop. I know there's not a reason in the world you should believe that, or Shawn should, but it's true."

"I believe it," he said, biting the lemon after giving it a squeeze into his tea. Some things are so familiar to me they catch me off guard. I had seen him do just that, order cold tea and bite into the lemon a thousand times. He always made the same face, part savoring the tart flesh of the fruit when it first hit his tongue and then part bitter shudder as the juice and pith made contact with his various taste buds. Something about that reaction was so much a part of my story that it caught my heart in a painful grip and I felt tears sting my eyes.

"Do you?" I asked hoarsely.

"Of course I do, Jordie," he said gently, causing my tears to fall freely. His brow furrowed. "What's this?" He reached over and put a hand on mine.

I shook my head and tried to get a grip. *Cooper.* Just seeing him made me feel safe. Loved in a way I felt from no one else. He made me want to be more and better, and he purified me in ways I couldn't begin to describe. The process was far from painless. Cooper was 100 percent true; so clean and shiny it hurt sometimes to look at him.

"I believe in you, Cooper," I told him. "If I've believed in nothing else in this world, I've always believed in you."

Cooper grinned at me. "Have you been at the Hallmark cards again?" He was teasing—as usual—trying to get me over my emotional meltdown, but I wasn't sure it was going to work. I wanted to tell him about Ken and about what had happened since I'd gotten to St. Nacho's. I told him about Ken's parents, and his brother Mark, and the terrible fight they'd had.

"Do you remember coming out to your parents?" he asked.

I rolled my eyes. "How could I forget it? I got a one-way trip to my Aunt Ally's farm, where she tried to straighten me out by making me work like a fucking slave."

"But eventually you came home," he reminded me. "Eventually your parents got over the shock and the fights, and your mom convinced your dad that you should be home with your family so you could finish out your final year of school."

"That cost her," I muttered, suddenly not as hungry as I had been before. "I think my dad broke her ribs. He let me come home so she wouldn't tell the police." I was so ashamed, I couldn't meet his eyes. "I never told you that."

"I knew," Cooper said softly. "He let you come home so *I* wouldn't tell the police. My dad and I... We were trying to keep an eye out for her. We always felt like we screwed up." Cooper swallowed hard. "I never told you either."

For a long moment I just stared at the best friend I ever had. "Well, for fuck's sake."

"What?"

"I never thought I could love you more." I got choked up again. "But now I do. Thanks a whole lot."

He gripped my hand over the table. "Sorry," he said, laughing a little. "Me too. I love you too. Welcome home."

I was crying in my napkin when the waiter came over with our food. Cooper casually told him that I'd just received the news that I was with child. I was so busy having a nervous breakdown, laughing and crying at the same time, that my food got cold before I had a chance to eat it.

One good thing about losing it completely in a restaurant outside of town is that when it's over you can take a walk on the beach, get it out of your system, and laugh at yourself.

We rode back down PCH, just the two of us on the almost empty road. The sky was covered with clouds, behind which the silver moon put out only enough light to ghost through occasionally, seeming to bob in the sky inside its faint halo. He pulled up just outside of my motel room and I got off the bike. I took the helmet off and handed it back, and he removed his, just so we could say good night.

The thing I always liked best about us—about Cooper and me—is that neither of us needed to speak to make ourselves understood. Not when we were kids, and apparently, not now. I stood for more than a minute, just drinking him in, the warmth of his gaze on me, the sweetness of his smile. He looked back at me the entire time, letting me know that it was still there between us, that magic that was our refuge.

"Go home," I said at last. "Say hi to Shawn for me."

He turned and roared off down the street, his taillight fading until it became another blur of memory.

## Chapter Fifteen

I pulled the motel key from my pocket and turned to open the door. Behind me a car pulled up, shining its lights on me and idling, the radio tuned loud. When the driver didn't cut the engine after a bit, I turned to find that it was Ken's Tahoe.

I waited to see whether he wanted to talk or just let his SUV glare at me for a while. Eventually he got out and made his way slowly to where I was standing with my back against the door.

"You aren't wasting any time," he remarked.

"What the hell is that supposed to mean?"

He had the grace to sort of deflate. "I went by the gym, and Izzie said you left early with some guy."

I sighed. "That was Cooper."

He toed the ground in front of his foot.

"Go home, Ken."

He let one of his crutches dangle on his forearm and put his hand on the door next to my head. The next thing I knew, he was kissing me, stepping into my body with his. Tiny sparks of electricity snapped wherever we touched, and it wasn't long before I was shaking with need. He pulled his lips away, and I was glad to see his eyes were dark and wide. Whatever was between us, we shared it. He still had me crushed to the door when he slid his hand down my arm to take the key from me.

"All right?" he asked before inserting the key in the lock. His eyes met mine, and they begged me to let him in. "Say it's all right, Jordan."

I nodded because I couldn't make my voice work. He keyed the door and we all but fell inside.

"This is crazy," I whispered. He lurched against me and steadied himself against the inside wall as he dropped his crutches and clung to me.

"You're so hot," he told me, slipping his hands beneath my clothes. "I want to feel your skin. Come here." Jackets and shirts hit the floor. I definitely heard a button pop off his shirt and ping against the cheap laminated dresser before it rolled under the bed and hit the wooden platform there. He was kissing me hard, fucking me with his mouth while he held on to me and edged me across the room. We nearly lost our balance then, but he gripped my ass with both hands and steadied himself somehow. We tottered in a move that was almost like a dance for a minute but remained upright.

I loved the soft little needy noises he made, how touching different parts of his body in new ways changed the pitch and tone. I was determined to learn him, to play him like an instrument, to become a prodigy and make him sing for me in ways he didn't even know he was capable of yet.

We hit the bed together, me backward and bending at the knee until I sat on the edge. He knelt around my thighs, straddling me. His dick seemed hard and huge against my belly, and he curled around me like a cat.

"Does it always feel like this?" he asked, pushing the hair back off my face, a gesture I found tender and at odds with his size. "When I'm with you, it's like I just get it right. There's a thousand baseball analogies…" He pushed me onto my back and started unbuckling my belt. "It's like that perfect *crack* sound a bat makes before a home run ball flies out of the park."

"Mmph," I said, because I could hardly get my brain in gear once he rubbed my dick with his hand. "Oh, *jeez.*"

"Like that?" he asked, pulling open the button-front fly of my jeans and digging my cock out of my briefs. "You want it too."

"Not really." I felt like being a shit.

"Liar." He flicked my dick with a finger and got a reaction he didn't expect when I gasped and leaked a pearly drop of precum onto his hand. "You like that?"

Caught out, I rolled my eyes.

"You *like* that!" He laughed at me. "Papi likes it rough."

Okay, yeah. It wasn't a secret, but I wasn't bound to share it with men I didn't trust. I knew Ken wasn't the type to hurt me, but looking in his eyes, I found definite signs of an answering kink. He was smiling enigmatically at me. *Fuck.* If he knew any more about my body, he'd own it completely.

He experimented briefly with another flick. I bit my lip. "Aw, this just makes my day," he told me, practically lifting me in those beefy arms of his and sliding us both farther up onto the bed. He loomed over me, shoving his pants down and awkwardly climbing out of them.

"What to do?" He sighed, an exaggerated, blowy kind of sigh, as he pulled his belt from his trousers. It was a long, drawn-out process, during which he didn't take his eyes off mine. And those eyes, blue, but darker now, shadowed around the edges with a smudgy ring and hungry-looking, pinned me right to the bed like a trophy deer on a wall.

I tried to say something, but the way he was looking at me made the sound come out thick and garbled. At last, I got out, "Guh-huh." It was the best I could do.

"Looks like I found the key," he said, taking his belt and cinching it around my wrists. He gave it a yank. It was tight, but it didn't cut off the circulation. I knew that I should never let anyone restrain me without a thorough understanding of the situation and the parameters. For my peace of mind, I needed some ground rules. I needed a safe word if I was going to sub, but I doubted if he'd know a sub wasn't a sandwich or even what a safe word was.

"If I say 'snowman,' you stop what you're doing, no questions asked, do you agree?"

He froze. "Do you think I'm going to hurt you?"

I shook my head. "No. It's just the way you play."

His hands dropped to his sides. "You 'play' like this often?" I couldn't see what was going on in his head, but suddenly the air crackled with tension. The mood had definitely changed from one of carefree sexual exploration to…what? I didn't know.

"I have, yes." I sat up, my wrists still bound, to lean back against the headboard.

"Is there no end to your accomplishments?" He sat back on his haunches.

I couldn't imagine what he meant by that, so I sat while he stewed. I sometimes forgot how young he was. At twenty-three I was in jail; you don't stay young in jail. It was obvious in this light. His soft brown hair looked shaggy from where I'd messed with it, and his frown deepened as I tried to decide what to say. He looked like a kid whose mentor had ridiculed him.

"Why does it matter?" I asked him. "I'm almost thirty years old; you can't expect me to be—"

"Inexperienced? Like me, you mean?" He started to untie my wrists, and I pulled my hands back to prevent him.

"I never said that."

"But it's obvious, isn't it? It would be different if you were tying me up."

I grinned.

"What?" he asked, not at all happy with me.

"I begin to see what kind of a competitor you must have been as an athlete."

He flopped onto his side, looking utterly defeated. "Must have been. Could have been. Never got the chance. Was."

"Oh, Ken." I sighed. "I'm sorry, man. I didn't mean it that way."

"It doesn't matter."

"Yes, it does," I told him. "It matters very much to me. It matters if what I said hurt you."

"It didn't. I just forget sometimes that this isn't new to you. I forget that I'm the one who just came out, whose parents think he's lost his mind, whose brother hates him. And then I think for what? So you can *play* with me?"

"Whoa!" I held up my hands, but I couldn't do that time-out thing because I was bound. "Snowman."

He shut his mouth and glared at me.

"Yeah, playing isn't new. Subbing isn't new. Sex isn't new. But you're new, Ken, and I swear to you it's a new kind of new."

"What the fuck does that even mean?" he growled, clamping a hand on the pillow and yanking it out from under my back.

What *did* I mean by that? "I don't know!" I snapped at him. "How the fuck should I know?"

He raised his eyebrows and cracked a hint of a smile. "Are you having an episode?" I was so glad to see his smile that I put my bound hands around his neck and kissed him. I enjoyed the way his blue eyes lost focus.

"It doesn't matter what happened before, Ken," I told him. "I'm telling you, truthfully, that how I want *you* is new."

"My parents think it's pity. Or remorse."

"You're kidding."

"They say you're trying to relieve your guilty conscience."

"So what, I'm hitting the hospitals? Trolling the meetings of chapters of MADD? Looking for people damaged by drunk drivers so that I can show them a good time?" I guess I made it sound funny, even though that was the last thing I was feeling.

"You make that sound like a bad thing," he teased. Then his eyes became serious. "Why else would you want me?"

"You think—" I got a grip. "Whatever your parents might think of me personally, they'd have to be awfully damned dense if they can't see why I'd want to be with you. I think a better question is what the hell do you see in me?"

"You *feel* good. *I* feel good when I'm with you. I tried to tell Mark, but he's so angry."

"I saw. I'm sorry about that. I really like him."

"He likes you too; he's just angry with me." Ken caught my hips and pulled me close, not urgent now, just slow and sensual, kneading the muscles of my ass and undulating against me. "Can we save the whole exotic play thing for another time? You feel like cool water right now and I need to drink up."

"You'll have to untie my hands," I said, removing them from around his neck.

He hesitated. "We can revisit this, yeah?"

I laughed and nodded. "Oh, hell yeah."

He slipped the belt off my wrists and pulled me to him. "Even if I am a pity fuck, you always make it worth my while." I didn't call him on it. I didn't stop him or try to argue with him. I let him have me. I melted into him and dripped over him and gave him everything I had to give. He knew it wasn't pity. No matter what his parents or his brother said. *He had to know that.*

He murmured, "Shit," when he finally pushed his cock into me as if I hadn't been begging for it—out loud—for quite a while. "Fucking feels like heaven."

"C'mere." I pulled him down to me for a punishing kiss, glad I was limber enough to do it. He positioned my arms, one by one above my head and took hold of my wrists in one of his hands, holding them down. I don't know why but it added something, and *fuck* if I didn't love the way his ass was rising and falling and his hips pushed against me as he slammed me into the mattress, all big man and sex and bunching muscles. I was breathless and shouting his name in minutes as he snapped his lower body into mine, triumphant, with a face like he'd knocked one out of the park, like sliding into home plate just under the tag.

He let my hands go and fell on me, and I wrapped my arms around him and cradled his head into my shoulder, rubbing my cheek against his hair. I could feel him whispering against my skin, but I couldn't hear what he said. I didn't figure I really needed to know.

Ken rolled us onto our sides, slipping out of me, pulling off and tossing the condom. He got up to pee, awkwardly moving across the room on his crutches, and a moment later came back with a damp towel over his arm to clean me up. I'd come all over my belly, and he swept the towel over my skin gently. Neither of us spoke. After a minute, he tossed the towel on the floor and wrapped himself around me from behind. I curled into him spoonwise and felt his lips brush the nape of my neck. It was as if he brushed them against my heart.

"Thank you," I murmured.

His lips traced my ear as he shook his head, still saying nothing. I was tired and drifting when I heard him begin to breathe deeply and evenly behind me. I fell, moments later, into a deep and dreamless sleep.

* * *

The following morning, I left the room at five thirty while Ken still slept. I left the key with him, figuring I could get a spare from the manager. When I got to Day-Use, this time walking along the road through fog that made it hard to see even fifty feet in front of me, I found Mark sitting on one of the cement blocks in the parking lot, smoking a cigarette. I walked straight up to him, snatched it out of his hand, and stomped it out on the ground.

"Hey!" he said, all attitude. "You've got no right to do that." He was going for the pack in his pocket when I caught his hand.

"Stop that. You're an *athlete*. You're out of your mind to smoke. Soccer players have to run like hell. You lose your wind, you lose your game."

"Doesn't fucking matter, does it? Anything could happen. Shit comes along and ruins *everything*. I don't know how Ken can stand to even look at you."

"He's plenty bitter," I told Mark as I sat down next to him on the block. "He just doesn't hold his accident against me personally."

He dropped his head back and looked at the eastern horizon. The sun was trying to break through the fog, and every so often you could catch a glimpse of it, something light and shiny in all that gray.

"He spent the night with you again last night."

I said nothing.

He turned to me with eyes full of pain. "Can't you just leave him alone? Now he's not going to care whether he ever gets better because he has you to look at him like he's okay the way he is."

"What was in that cigarette you were smoking?" I asked. "He's not going to give up because I'm here to look at him...however I look at him. He's a tough contender, and he's getting back to his feet after a bad fucking fall. Ken is working every bit as hard as he can. What's the matter with you?"

"*You're* the matter. He talked about getting out there and trying to play ball again! Now he's buying a house here in St. Nacho's because he's into you, and it's like he's planning to grow old and die here. Like he wants to get a job at the Safeway bagging our groceries. Since you came, he's ready to settle for a whole lot less than he's ever really wanted."

I thought about that. "You really think so?"

"Yeah." He stared at me defiantly. "Look. I like you, you seem nice, but—"

"But not for your brother." I wasn't sure, but I thought maybe this approach, one that took him seriously, might have shocked him a little.

"Yeah." He looked at me, expecting me to argue.

"I haven't known your brother for very long," I told him. "But he strikes me as obstinate. A little competitive."

"He is." Mark hunched up as if he remembered a painful ordeal. "Don't ever tell him you know something he doesn't know. And don't ever play cards with him, and if you do, don't ever win."

"Seems like you know him pretty well."

"I ought to; he's my brother. He always has to win at everything. He always has to be first and best and biggest. One time, my mom said I might grow to be taller than him someday, and when she turned her back, he whispered that if I did, he'd snap me like a twig."

I laughed, but I hoped Ken was kidding at the time. "He sounds like a pretty determined guy."

"That's why I don't understand what's wrong with him. I don't understand why he's giving up on his dreams!" Mark was less agitated and maybe even softening toward me, treating me like someone with whom he could find answers rather than someone to blame. I hoped I could say something that would change his attitude toward his brother, because I thought Mark's defection hurt Ken more than anything else had.

Just then a minivan drove into the parking lot and pulled into one of the spaces. A woman got out, and even if Mark hadn't jerked guiltily, I would have recognized her as Ken's mother the minute I saw her. She had Ken's brown hair, although it was laced with silver, and his blue, blue eyes. She was pretty but carried extra weight that she didn't need. She shut the car door with a bang and walked with confidence, wearing black jeans and a long-sleeved T-shirt with sheepskin boots. There was so much of her in Ken, I wondered if Ken's father had any influence at all.

"I'm Ken's mother, Lydia Ashton." She seemed pleasant enough.

I wiped my damp hands on my trousers and stood. "Pleased to meet you," I said. She took my hand and shook it; her eyes were warm. I had no idea what to expect.

"I'm pleased to meet you too, Jordan," she said. I had no warning that she had an agenda at all.

"I know it must have been shocking when Ken told you about me; I mean that he's—"

"Gay?" she preempted me. "It wasn't the best day of my life, but it wasn't the worst."

"I see." By this time, I was bracing myself. Her calm demeanor was no longer fooling me. This woman hated me.

"I have no problem with Ken being gay, Jordan. I have a problem with him choosing an older man who has a prison record and needed to spend time in rehab. I have a problem with him choosing a drifter who has no family to speak of and only moved here because a couple of his friends work in the kitchen of a local gay bar."

I remained silent. For some reason, I couldn't figure out what to do with my hands. I tucked them under my armpits, holding myself together by sheer force of will while she talked.

"I'm sure you probably understand exactly what I'm talking about. Ken hit rock bottom during his accident. He's not the man he was. The man he was before the accident would not have chosen *you*, and I have to ask myself if you're good enough for him now."

"Mom," Mark said, but she held up a hand.

"Cut him loose," she told me. "I'm not here to be a bitch to you personally. I don't even know you. If you really care about him, if you really see how it is with him, you'll understand that he can't start something with you. He can't give you anything. If he tries, it will come from the energy he needs right now to get well."

"You make a pretty good argument."

"It's not an argument. It's the truth. If you stay with him, when he gets well he won't need you anymore anyway. You have to know that. You've probably experienced it. He'll resent you because you saw him at his worst. When he does eventually fall for someone, it will be someone who didn't see him when he was down."

"Mom," Mark began again. I could see his need to defend his brother—to defend me—at war with his own feelings on the subject. He saw what he perceived as injustice and stood up. I really, *really* liked this kid. "That's not like Ken."

She turned to him. "What *is* Ken like?" she asked him. She turned back to me. "I don't know him anymore. I just know that he can't be what you want. He won't be, even if he tries. I'm betting if you walk away, it will benefit him not just in the long run, but right away. He won't like it, but he doesn't have to like it. So my question for you is, do you care about my son? If you really care about him, then I'm sorry for it, but I still say cut him loose." She turned and walked away. She didn't even look back to see if Mark would follow her, but he started to do just that. He turned and shot me a look that I thought held regret.

"Jordan..." he said, holding his hands out palms up. "I'm sorry."

I shook my head. "It's fine. Go on ahead; you should see if you can get a ride to school."

He nodded and took off after his mom.

## Chapter Sixteen

I was still standing in the parking lot of Day-Use when Izzie drove up in her clown car. She got out, hefting a number of small weighted balls and an exercise mat. I helped her to grab some of it when she balanced it all in her arms and tried to use her remote to lock her car. I walked her to the door; she was unusually silent as she stuck her key in the lock.

"What's wrong?" she asked the minute we were inside, before she even turned on the lights. "You look like you've lost your best friend."

"Is it that obvious?"

"To me it is. Your aura looks like a bruise."

"Ken's mother was here."

"What?" Izzie turned to me. "Lydia was here? Really?"

"Yeah. She didn't stay long. Just long enough to tell me to go fuck myself."

"She did not!" Izzie dropped the balls on the floor and grabbed the lapels of my jacket. It was a little like being mauled by a declawed tiger.

"She did." I removed her hands gently. "She was very nice and got straight to the point. Her baby's gay, and she's fine with that. I'm just not good enough for him. I'm not what he needs. I'm not what he'd choose, and if it hadn't been for the accident, he never would have looked at me twice. It's all right. I've got to clean the men's room." I turned away from her to get the cleaning supplies.

"Jordan!"

I looked back. "It's really okay. She's right."

"Even if she was right, he *did* have that accident and he *is* looking at you." She came right up after me, clasping my shoulder in her strong grip. "I don't know how to explain it to you. He looks at you and undergoes a physical and emotional change. You're the KeyMaster."

My face heated up. "I am not," I told her. "He wants me because he knows he can have me."

"That's a major oversimplification. He saw you and right away he was attracted. Genuinely interested. He wanted you."

"How could he want me? He doesn't know the first thing about me."

"What did he need to know other than that you make him feel good?"

"Izzie, I'm the first out gay man he's been in contact with since the accident. It's not about me; it's about not hiding it anymore. It's about giving in to the temptation that years of being an athlete and trying to live up to his parents' expectations didn't allow him to even consider."

"Is that what you really think?" came Ken's appalled voice behind me. *Oh shit.* "What the *fuck*?"

He came toward me on his crutches, stiff, I thought, from anger and the chill of the morning. "Ken, I—"

"I'm not about to try to convince you," he snapped at me.

"Ken." Izzie stepped in, her brow furrowed. "I'm sure what Jordan meant was—"

"I know exactly what Jordan meant," Ken told her. He turned around and headed for the door. "He meant stop acting like a lovesick dog and find someone else to bother."

"Don't you dare put words into my mouth, Ken Ashton," I shouted, but he was halfway out the door. He didn't turn back.

Izzie came up right behind me and gave me a hard shove. "Go after him, what's the matter with you?"

"I will not," I told her. "He's right. He needs to look elsewhere. I'm not right for everything a guy like him has to offer."

"*Jordan.*"

"Do I still work here?" I asked her, feeling defiant and stupid and brokenhearted all at once.

"Of course you still work here." She sighed. I think she was a little hurt, but I didn't acknowledge it in any way.

"Then I need to clean the men's room," I said and picked up my basket of supplies. I left her there, gazing out at the parking lot where Ken was getting into his car. I could imagine his pain. I felt it in my gut. But what he needed most right then was not to square off against his entire family over what his mother had *rightly* called the wrong guy. I wasn't about to start a relationship. I was lucky enough to have a few good friends, and I was losing them, if Izzie's face was anything to go by, faster than I could make them.

Cooper's image popped into my head as it often did when I was feeling emotionally off-kilter. Cooper once cared about me enough to save my life. Not from a burning building or a speeding car, but Cooper had been there for me at my worst moment, a time when I realized that I either had to keep putting one foot in front of the other or end it all. That had scared the hell out of me, and I'd had Cooper's strong arms to hold me. I'd had his love to sustain me. I would never, ever forget that.

I wished that Ken had someone like that. Someone who could buoy him up when he was in trouble and keep him from drowning in his doubts and fears. It couldn't be me. My very existence in his life was like an anchor dragging him down, and not because he was gay. His mother was right; I was not the man for him. Nothing could make me worthy of the trust he'd placed in me. I'd already violated that by letting him believe we had more than we could ever have together.

I wasn't about to go after him or call him. I wasn't about to take it back. Izzie may be certain our auras matched, and our chemistry might work for a while, but eventually, even if he didn't want to, he'd begin to see my white trash ex-con ass for what it was. I poured myself into cleaning the bathroom, still smarting from Ken's angry words.

Izzie broke into my thoughts. "Ken has an appointment today to get a massage. What am I supposed to tell him?"

"I don't think that's a good idea."

"You won't even work on him? Isn't the point that he be given the best care possible?"

"Yes it is, and when he's in here and my hands are all over him, and he's lying there thinking I'm punishing him, wishing he'd get lost or whatever, how is he going to feel?"

"Just because his mother said—"

"Izzie." I put the rag and spray bottle I was using down on the long countertop and gave her my full attention. I must have looked a mess, standing there wearing rubber gloves, sweaty from scrubbing tile. "His mother has nothing to do with this. He doesn't have the first clue what he wants. He's not even experienced enough to ask for it. He's coming back from a tragedy, and his body and brain are seriously messed up. I don't want him to get swept off his feet by the first guy that comes along and offers him hot sex any more than she does."

"You don't believe in love at first sight?"

"Of course not. I think that's a fairy tale that leads even intelligent people to drive-through Vegas weddings and morning-after divorces."

"You don't believe it happens? People say it happens. When they go on television and say, 'it was love at first sight,' you think they're not telling the truth?"

"What I think is," I said, wishing I had a free hand to rub my face because my throat hurt and it was making my nose run, "I *think* that it may happen to some people, maybe. But not to me."

"How do you know?" she almost whispered. "Never mind that you're not in love; how do you know that you couldn't be someone a guy falls in love with at first sight? How do you know that Ken doesn't love you?"

I didn't address whether I was in love. Something about that didn't bear scrutiny. "I'm not the kind of guy you fall in love with. He knows nothing about me; he can't possibly love me."

"Maybe not intellectually, Jordan, but other things play a part and—"

"I don't deserve it, Izzie," I told her, flinging the gloves off. The moist air was starting to get to me. The bathroom was claustrophobic at the best of times, but now, when I was already agitated, it felt like there was no air to breathe. "When Ken falls in love, I hope to hell that person is a better man than I am. Look. I'm done here for now. I've got to go. I need to..." I started to pile all the supplies back into the basket.

I could see Izzie was defeated. She looked at me with a kind of motherly concern that I didn't think I could justify right then. "Take some time. You've been here long hours since you came. Take the day."

"Thank you, Izzie." I swallowed hard. "I think maybe I'll...maybe I'll take a drive."

"Be careful." Izzie took the basket from me. "We'll be here when you get back. Don't give up on St. Nacho's."

I felt a tug on my heart as I looked at her. "I won't. I like it here."

"Good," she said. "You get on now."

I looked at my watch as I left Day-Use; it wasn't even seven thirty a.m. yet. As I walked home, I looked over each one of the businesses on the street. I already felt like I belonged here. I saw my coffee place and the Chinese joint that stayed open late. I'd gotten soap to use at the Laundromat and eaten at the Denny's. If I wanted to stay in town, it was going to be necessary to keep to myself. Even the tiniest bit of involvement could disrupt the delicate balance I was trying to maintain.

St. Nacho's wanted to claim me, and I wanted to belong here. I didn't want anything to mess that up.

I got in my car and took off without even going inside my motel room. I took the Pacific Coast Highway heading south and finally decided that what I really wanted was to stand on a beach all by myself. I wanted to find a high place to look at the water, to see how far I could see out to the horizon. I needed a sunset.

I wasn't trying to figure everything out. I planned to simply sit somewhere that would remind me of how insignificant I was. Being unimportant in the vast scheme of things has its perks. One of them is the sure and certain knowledge that whatever Ken's feelings were for me or mine for him, I would be forgotten as soon as the next guy came along.

Sure, that made me sad. It made me feel like shit. When Ken talked about feeling right? Well, I'd felt it. More than right. In that complex blend of emotions I felt when I was around him was what I might call *inevitable*. He gave me peace that filled me up and overflowed me until all I wanted was to be the guy standing by his side for as long as he would let me. But I knew I could find peace alone as well, and that it would be better for everyone—but especially Ken—in the long run if I did.

I climbed down a rocky path on a deserted part of the coast where I could see several shallow depressions filled with seawater and teeming with colorful organisms. The water was icy cold, and after even a few minutes my feet began to sting a little as I groped around. Coming from Wisconsin to California, I'd learned to love the ocean. It's a vast wilderness of which only limited parts can be seen, unveiled, as in the case of tidal pools, every so often like a special treat.

Farther out in the water, waves churned a gray-green, flushing sand and other debris around so I couldn't see what was underneath it even as close as six feet away. But in the pools I could find and even touch starfish, sea urchins, crabs, sea sponges, and other kinds of spiny things and crustaceans I couldn't name.

I let the ocean breeze blow away my anxiety. I let the rippling water in the tidal pools soothe my spirit. I stayed there all day, glad I always carried sunscreen, water, and a variety of clothes in the trunk of my car. I watched the sun slip down toward the water on the horizon. At one point, it was in one part of the sky and the moon in another. That seemed so startling to me, and beautiful, that I felt it catch on something inside my heart that held it there long after the sun was gone. I made my way back to St. Nacho's, certain of the place I held in the world and my responsibility to maintain it.

\* \* \*

When I got back, I went to the motel's cramped office to change rooms at the SeaView Motel. I wasn't proud of it, but I was desperate to move to a room to which Ken did not possess a key. I didn't plan to hide from him exactly; I just didn't want to be instantly available. I found myself telling the bored night manager that I'd given my key to someone and they hadn't given it back. He made me pay twenty-five dollars for the lost key, even though I told him I was sure to get it back. He gave me a look that said he didn't believe me. I couldn't tell whether he was serious.

"Perhaps," the night clerk began, studying me in an assessing way that I found rude but not unexpected, "you should refrain from bringing strangers back to your room."

"And suck the joy out of my carefree homosexual lifestyle?" I guess I felt like being an asshole. "Hardly."

He raised his eyebrows. "Well, I never." Jeez. Did people really say that?

"I have between eleven and twelve on Friday night open, if you want to," I informed him as I left. The bells on the door gave an irritating jingle. I jerked the door again to ring them harder. "Don't bother to dress."

I actually heard him laugh before I shut the door behind me. Apparently he was an old curmudgeon but didn't particularly hate me. Not enough to kick me out of his motel, anyway.

I was about to enter my room with the manager's spare key to get my things, and I had just pushed the key into the lock when I heard footsteps come up behind me. I turned to look, frankly expecting to see Ken. What I saw instead was a black flashlight, the kind that cops carry, coming at me with such speed I couldn't hope to dodge it. As I heard it crack into the bone on the side of my head, I thought, "Oh, *fuck*."

## Chapter Seventeen

I remember the accident I *caused*, the one that killed Bobby Johnson, in exact detail. I remember, first of all, that flash of disbelief when I couldn't believe what my senses told me. I heard the onlookers shouting without understanding them, like they were monkey noises from the zoo, and from that moment forward everything came at me in slow motion. The terror of that day still hadn't left me, and to say that my heart stopped or maybe imploded in my chest felt like a vast understatement.

If I took all the disappointment and sadness and shock of my life and added it together, it could never equal what I felt in that first sickening minute after I ran over Bobby Johnson with my truck.

Following on the heels of that, a kind of madness took over. First, I'd wanted to deny everything. I was desperate to find an excuse or a reason or a plan to escape responsibility. Then I had the almost irresistible surge of desire to flee. It still sounds trite, but if I could have switched places with Bobby I would have, if only to escape that wrenching guilt.

For the first few minutes after I was attacked at the SeaView Motel, I thought there might even have been some magical shift in time and space that had granted me my wish, because the events of that long-ago night were so similar, starting with the flashing lights.

"Jordan." Someone seemed to be calling my name from a long way off. There was a light shining in my eyes, bouncing back and forth, irritating me, then being pulled away a moment later. "Jordan, is that your name? Jordan?"

I couldn't answer, but I heard feet moving. Something heavy banged down on the concrete next to my head. I heard wheels squeaking and the chatter of police radios. Something teased at my memory about the police. I shifted my eyes to look for Bill, Cooper's brother-in-law, hoping that if I was in trouble again, he could explain it to me. Bill was a good man, a man I'd come to respect and love like family. A face appeared in my field of vision but it wasn't Bill's, and what I could see was blurry.

"Jordan," came a voice I recognized, but not Bill's. "Jordan, it's me, Andy."

I looked to where I thought I heard the voice. *Not Bill.* Andy. Bill was back in River Falls, and I was in St. Nacho's. Andy. Officer Andrew, Izzie's boyfriend. My vision was blurry and my head... What the fuck was wrong with my head?

"Jordan, if you can hear me, can you squeeze my hand?" I felt him touch my hand. He laid his own on it, palm down. I tried to give it a squeeze, but I didn't know if he felt it. Nothing seemed real. I felt like a ghost. I could see them, I could hear them, but I couldn't respond. I couldn't let them know I was there.

My eyes were watering, and I felt the tears leak down the sides of my face into my ears. The distance I felt from the scene—from the tense faces looking at me—and my inability to make myself understood combined to confuse me. Was I crying? I couldn't tell. There was other wetness on the side of my head, on my neck, and I had to think hard what it might mean. EMTs waved bloody gloves in my field of vision as they put a neck support on me and bandaged my head. I slipped further and further away from the sight and the sound of the people around me.

I caught one last look at Andy, and what I saw there scared the crap out of me. What must I look like if he looked at me like that? Like I was already gone. I tried again to squeeze his hand. He felt something, I think, and peered closely at me in the light given off by the headlights of the police cars.

"Jordan," he said gently, brushing a tear from my cheek. "Don't fret. We've got you." He looked grim. I took that to mean that things were not good.

I couldn't talk; it was useless.

"Did you see who hit you?"

I remained silent, mesmerized by everything that was going on around me. Sometimes it seemed to speed up and sometimes it was excruciatingly painful and slow.

"You'll be okay, son," Andy told me as I felt myself hoisted up onto a gurney.

I wanted Cooper. I wanted to tell Cooper…something. I wished I could see Ken. But that wasn't right. I couldn't see Ken. He needed… He didn't need someone like me.

I didn't let Andy's hand go when he tried to pull it away, and his gaze shot back to my face. I moved my mouth, incapable of anything but the puff of breath that escaped.

"I'll call Izzie, Jordan. She'll know what to do."

*Not Ken!* I wanted to shout. Finally, my stomach gave a sickening lurch as the EMTs lifted the gurney and rolled it to the ambulance. I had a moment's terror when I thought I'd vomit, and then…nothing.

\* \* \*

When I woke in the hospital, I had no idea how long I'd been there. The fact that I couldn't tell what time it was—or even what day—was frightening. It was daytime. I could tell from the way light filtered through the vertical blinds. The room I was in wasn't private but mine was the last bed, near the windows, and even with the curtain drawn between me and whoever was in the next bed, I knew someone was there from the steady, rattling breaths they took and the sound of a heart monitor.

I was hooked up to an IV and something felt weird about my dick. I had bandages on my head and from the feel, stitches or staples. I tried my voice, but my tongue was dry and felt like sandpaper. I pried my mouth open and found I could only croak. I looked around and saw a Call button on the pillow next to me, but I was too weak to press it.

I closed my eyes and drifted again. I have no idea if anyone came to check on me. I fell back into a sound sleep. I dreamed of police cars and flashlights. I dreamed that I was lying on the ground and the EMTs were working on me.

That irritating light was dancing in my eyes again, only this time when I looked at it closely, instead of seeing it being pulled away I saw a police flashlight coming down on my head to crush it.

I gasped and jerked, giving a hard tug on the IV line that was still attached to my hand. My head exploded with pain and my vision swam.

"Jordan." I heard a woman's voice. "It's me. Don't tug your arm, okay? It's got the IV thing in it and you'll tear something."

"Izzie," I said, barely whispering the words through horribly chapped lips.

"Oh, honey." Izzie ran a fingertip over the back of my hand. "Someone hit you over the head."

"Why?" If I had been back home, I wouldn't have needed to ask. But here in St. Nacho's? I didn't remember doing anything worthy of that kind of attack. I hadn't been in town long enough to piss anyone off that badly.

"I don't know." Izzie sounded close to tears.

"Was it…Ken?" I thought I'd prepared myself for the answer to that question, but as soon as the question left my mouth, I realized I hadn't even prepared myself to ask it. It was going to hurt if Ken had done this to me. I knew I'd made him angry, knew I'd hurt him. But damn, if he'd done this to me, I wouldn't know what to do.

"It wasn't Ken. Hell no," Izzie said. "That was a vicious assault; I know Ken would never do anything like that."

"I know. I didn't really… I thought maybe—"

"No, Jordan. I know Ken would never do this; the police are still trying to find out who did. It looks like an ordinary robbery. Someone took your car and your wallet."

I almost laughed, but everything hurt too much. What a joke. A ten-year-old car and a wallet with nothing in it but a couple of twenties. If they searched my room, they might have found the rest of my cash.

"The room?" I mumbled. Even that amount of talking was making me sick to my stomach.

"No, I don't think so. Andy said they didn't have time. The night clerk in the motel saw a man running and then someone drove your car out of the parking lot at top speed. He thought it was you and came out to have a look around to see if you did any damage, and that's when he found you. Andy said the EMTs think you're lucky he did."

"Oh, fuck, Izzie." I was drowning in pain and my vision was getting worse. "Call the doctor. I can't...blurry...my right eye." My fingers tingled and there was a funny metallic taste in my mouth. Izzie wavered in my field of vision, such as it was, and the last thing I saw was the expression of fear on her face as she grabbed up the Call button for the nurses' station.

* * *

I woke the next time to find Cooper dozing in a chair near my bed. I stared at him for a while. I no longer heard the breathing of the other patient in the room. It seemed ominous. I lay there trying to be as quiet as possible, worrying that something awful was on the other side of that curtain. Eventually I outsmarted myself and was forced to take a deep, shuddering breath. Cooper's eyes fluttered open at the sound.

"Hey," he said in a low, soft voice, his head still resting on his hand. He shifted a little, leaning in. Something about the dark and the quiet must have affected him; I don't suppose there was really any reason to whisper, except it seemed to be the thing to do.

I still didn't completely grasp what was happening to me. I'd heard snatches of conversations and opened my eyes to see the faces of people I didn't know. Doctors and nurses woke me up to ask me questions, take blood, or stick me with needles. Waking up to find Cooper next to me was like the sun shining through a bad storm. Once again, I was in trouble and he was by my side.

"Hey," I whispered back. "The fuck happened to me?"

"You were mugged," Cooper offered with a shrug.

"Mugged." I tried to imagine. "That's what I get for coming to the big city."

Cooper looked at me to see if I was kidding. I don't think he believed I was until I cracked a painful smile. He was still so beautiful. He lowered his lashes sleepily and grinned. I took in the familiar planes of his face, his piercings, and the barbell in his eyebrow. I could make out the tat on his neck. Just seeing him was reassuring.

"Scary in here. Where's my roommate?"

"Went home," he told me. "You've been out of it for a couple of days."

"Jeez." It was frightening that time had passed without me realizing. "I'm Rip van Winkle. Do they have flying cars yet?"

Cooper made a shushing sound. "You don't need to joke, Jordie. I know how scared you are." He brushed a finger along my arm.

"I'm glad you're here," I told him. "I'm sorry. You always have to—"

"Don't." Cooper cut me off. "I'm here. Izzie called. She told me that we should take turns so you always had someone you knew here when you woke up."

My chapped lips were cracking, and it hurt to try to talk. "That's nice."

"I should call Andrew Callahan. He wanted to know when you could answer questions."

"Don't call him. I'm not ready yet." I thought back to that moment—so shocking—when I was attacked. "How bad am I hurt?"

"They didn't tell me. Izzie was crazy with worry, though. She said she was here and you had a seizure."

"I don't remember," I murmured.

"No, I don't suppose so." He reached over and pressed the nurses' station Call button. "Maybe someone can answer your questions. If I were you I'd want answers."

"Thank you," I whispered. I still felt too weak to lift my arms and signal for myself. What was wrong with me? I could hardly stay awake. I was starting to get that panicky feeling, almost as though I were being buried alive, like there was no air and no way out.

I was breathing in a jerky, frantic way that was bound to lead to hyperventilation when a young-looking Latino walked into the room in a turquoise scrub shirt and pants. "Hey. You're awake."

I looked up at him, wondering who he was.

"What's the matter?" he asked, his dark brown eyes full of concern. "Calm down, Jordan. Can I call you Jordan? I'm Mike." He took my wrist and checked my pulse. "You're racing a little. Is something worrying you?"

I nodded. "I feel scared," I told him. I was embarrassed for Cooper to hear it. For some reason, whenever I closed my eyes I could see that flashlight coming down on my head, and my breathing sped up. It was as if I could hear the sickening crunch of metal on bone all over again. My heart started to slam against my rib cage, and I felt my skin crawl. "If I close my eyes I—"

"Shh." Cooper reached out a hand and squeezed my arm to slow me down.

"I'm okay," I said automatically, although it was a lie. "Just a little scared... I keep thinking about it. When I close my eyes."

"I understand that's pretty common," said Mike. "When people have accidents or suffer an assault, I think that it's normal to relive it for a while, and it can feel pretty real. I'll tell the doctor, though, that you're having these feelings. Did they just start?"

"I don't know. I was fine... Then—" Mike was rubbing my hand gently. It was something to focus my attention on. "Then I felt... I couldn't breathe."

"You had a substantial blow to the head. You have a concussion. You remember the incident?"

I nodded. My problem seemed to be that I couldn't forget it.

"In the morning, the doctor will explain everything. You've been in and out of consciousness for several days."

"Several?" I looked at Cooper.

He nodded.

I looked toward the window. "I can't tell the time."

"It's nighttime," Mike said. "Three in the morning. The doctor will see you as soon as he can."

Even that small interaction exhausted me. I was drifting off before Mike left the room. "Cooper? My memory is for shit. How come they let you stay in here at this hour?"

"I think they're cutting us some slack for Izzie and Andrew."

"Yeah?" That was nice. "You can go home, you know."

"I know." He leaned his head back over his hand. "I just don't want you to wake up alone. Izzie will be here in a bit."

"Thanks." I didn't know what I ever did to deserve my friends. I barely lifted my hand off the bed, but he gave it a gentle squeeze. "I owe you, man."

"Damned right you do." He grinned and tucked his head down. It wasn't long before I was drifting off again.

* * *

I dreamed I was in the hospital and Cooper was sitting beside me, just as he had been; only it was the middle of a busy day. People walked up and down the corridors in squeaky shoes, their feet making louder noises than I remembered. I heard gurney wheels rattle and squeak and the sound of machinery, all the beeps of monitors and the occasional alarm.

I was in a hospital gown, and I recall thinking it was drafty, but I woke up with the sense that I had to find something, so I had gotten up and gone to look for it. In the dream, Cooper was sound asleep, and gentle touches didn't wake him. He had his head on his hand, and I just rose and walked past him somehow, magically free of all the tubes and monitoring devices that tethered me to the bed.

It was as if I were invisible. I passed the nurses' station, and Mike was there with two other people in scrubs. They talked together quietly, not even aware that I was listening in. They were joking about the doctors, the patients, and the charts and jovially imagining they could run the whole show. I walked past them and got on the elevator, which seemed to require an interminably long time to take me to the first floor. The Muzak was intolerable.

When the doors opened, instead of being in the hospital, the elevator deposited me onto the beach at St. Nacho's, just in front of Nacho's Bar. I walked past the bar, determined that I had to do something, or find something. My feet carried me across the sand first, then the pavement, down highways, past pastureland, farms, and lakes. I wasn't surprised to find myself walking on the main road into River Falls. It seemed the most natural thing to amble down Main Street, past Mama Lina's and Hallowed Grounds, past

Veterans Park and into the tract homes around the university.

I wasn't even surprised when I found myself walking up to the door of the Johnsons' house, where I rapped just below the brass knocker that was inscribed with THE JOHNSON FAMILY. I was shocked when Bobby answered the door, his tiny body perfect and whole. I found the heavy cast metal flashlight someone used to hit me in my hand.

"Here," I said and held it out for him.

He opened his tiny, perfect mouth and screamed.

* * *

I jerked awake like I was shot out of a cannon. "Fuck," I muttered. "Fuck, fuck, fuck."

Beside me in a chair, dressed primly in a pair of khaki pants and a blouse with a soft pink sweater tied around her shoulders, sat my mother. "You are going to have to do something about that language. This is a *hospital,* Jordie." She said the word *hospital* reverently, in hushed tones, like she would say priest if we were Catholic.

"*Mom?*"

"Hi, baby." She looked around. "I got here while you were asleep. I didn't want to wake you, so I thought…"

"How did you get here?" I noticed shadows under her eyes. There was a faint bruise on her jaw. I knew if I looked at her wrists, which were covered by her demure white blouse, I'd find more bruises. My father was more of a restrainer than a hitter. He restrained, he harangued, and usually, my mother gave in before he started hitting.

She swallowed hard. "I came on a plane," she evaded. It wasn't as though she didn't know I meant *how did you get away from Dad?* She knew. She chose not to answer. "That nice young friend of yours picked me up all the way in San Francisco last night and brought me here."

*Couldn't be Cooper.* My mother wasn't the type to jump on the back of a motorcycle. "Shawn?"

"Hm? No, Ken. The boy with the canes," she said. "He was very nice. He couldn't carry my bags, so he paid for someone to carry them and put them in the car."

"Ken brought you here?" Why did that make me feel...? What did that make me feel? *Warm, maybe.*

"I met Izzie, your boss." My mother smiled. "You've made a very good impression on her. She had the airline ticket waiting for me at the airport in St. Paul. I saw Cooper and Shawn."

I could still hardly take it in. My mother was sitting next to me in St. Nacho's. I'd been mugged and bashed on the head, true, but I was pretty sure this wasn't a dream. "My head hurts," I told her.

She put a soothing hand out and brushed the side of my face with the knuckles on the back of her hand. She was careful. I could tell from her eyes that I still looked like hell.

"My poor baby," she sighed, and everything melted away until it was just her fingers and me, and I was maybe two again. When I was a kid, she used to follow this up with, "You have to do everything the hard way, don't you?" Back in the day, it was true.

"I swear, Mom, I was working hard, making friends... I was being nice and trying to be useful—"

She shushed me. "I know, Jordie. I know."

I felt desperate to make her understand. "I don't think this time it was entirely my fault."

"Shh, baby," she said. "We'll sort it out." After a while I was too tired to move, and I fell asleep with her hand in mine.

## Chapter Eighteen

"You, my friend," Mike told me as he rolled me out to the parking area in a wheelchair, "will be missed."

"Thank you." My head was bandaged; part of it was shaved. My balance was for shit, but the doctor told me that would pass. I had, in the two weeks I'd been in the hospital, gotten dramatically better. I was still tired all the time, and the expectation was that I'd be homebound for close to a month before I could work again.

I probably wouldn't have any long-term complications, but I wouldn't be allowed to drive in California for a year because of a mandatory reporting law, and only then if I was free of seizures during that time. My doctors weren't sure whether I'd have another, and I could develop epilepsy. I was bound to be unsteady on my feet and weak for a while.

My mom walked alongside my wheelchair. She was coming back with me to the SeaView motel, and we had plans to stay there for a while until we figured out where I could go. She wanted me to go home to River Falls while I recovered. For a lot of very good reasons, I refused.

In Shawn's Camry on the way to the motel, she started again.

"I still think if you were to come home, just for a month or two while you get back on your feet—"

There was no way I was going home to my father's house, and now, after seeing my mother for the past week, I hoped she wouldn't go either. "There's no reason I can't just stay here. My follow-up appointments are all here. I have work. I could just do half days for a while at first, but—"

"How are you going to afford to stay in that motel while you're only working part-time? What about the hospital costs?"

"I have health insurance," I said. It hadn't been very good health insurance, and it cost a bundle, but I was so glad I'd been smart enough to get it. What, if anything, it covered I had no idea. I was embarrassed to tell her Izzie had passed the hat at Day-Use and come up with enough money for a month's rent. To hear her tell it, food would be falling from the sky and people were standing in line to take me to my doctor appointments. I recognized the frenzy of activity around an injured hometown boy from growing up in River Falls. I didn't feel like I deserved that kind of consideration, but they all made me feel very cared for.

"My rent is paid for the next month. Izzie told me not to worry about that at all. We can stay there and pretend we're on vacation. We could go to the beach." I knew I'd caught her. A flicker of something that looked very much like yearning passed over her face when I said the word *beach*. "It's cold out, but no matter the time of year it's beautiful."

She snorted. "Cold."

"Have you talked to Dad?" I asked. We were both sitting in the backseat of Shawn's car, and even so, she blushed guiltily.

"Hush," she said.

"Mom," I reminded her. "Shawn can't hear us."

"It's just not—"

"I know. It's not something you talk about. I got that."

"No." She looked at her hands. "I was going to say, 'not something I want to talk about *right now.*'"

I looked closely at her. Maybe St. Nacho's was having its renowned magical effect on her too. It was true that in the week she'd been here, she'd blossomed. I'd never seen her so carefree. Not even when I was young, before my father's occasional drinking and verbal abuse had escalated to nightly terror and the atmosphere in our home ground us both down to dirt. In St. Nacho's, where she had no one watching everything she did and waiting to pounce on her and make her feel useless, my mother had become lovely and serene. Younger-looking than she had been, even before I went to prison. I was enjoying the calm between us when I realized that Shawn had passed by the motel.

"Shawn," I said stupidly, forgetting that he couldn't hear me. I motioned for him in the mirror, but he ignored me. I don't know if he could tell I was trying to get his attention or not. More than once I'd suspected Shawn of ignoring something, not because he was unaware of it, but because he chose to. I was on the passenger side of the car and chose not to tap his shoulder in case it might startle him.

"What is it?" my mother asked me as I sat back in defeat.

"This isn't the way to the motel." I watched as we passed landmarks I knew to be farther on the outskirts of town. When we passed the high school, I had the feeling I'd been on that particular road before.

"Maybe he has an errand to run."

"I don't know…"

"Is it something we should be worried about?" My mother frowned.

"No, I'm sure Shawn will explain," I said with more confidence than I felt. I had a tremendous headache, and all I could think was that I hoped there wasn't going to be some sort of party. When we turned on a street with a more rural look to it, everything clicked into place. Moments later, we pulled up in front of the house Ken had shown me.

"Why are we here?" my mother asked.

"I don't know." I felt completely incapable of the argument I knew was coming. I couldn't stay here. Even if I were so inclined, my mother couldn't be expected to live in a house with things that crawled and crept. She couldn't be expected to do the kind of cleaning that Ken's house required just to make it livable. When Shawn pulled to a stop, he climbed out. He let my mother out first, and together they came around to get me.

"Shawn," I said, taking his hand and making certain I had his attention. "I don't know what Ken told you, but—"

Shawn put his hand to my mouth to stop me talking and then motioned with his head to acknowledge Ken, who stood on the front steps, which looked to have been shored up since I was last there. At least he wasn't falling through them. He came down the stairs one foot at a time on each, using his new canes. It was good seeing this obvious evidence that he was making progress. When he reached my mother and me, he stopped. Shawn was pulling the plastic bag with my things from the hospital out of the passenger seat.

"Ken," I began. "I'm sure you mean well—"

"Come inside," he said abruptly and turned. I looked at my mom, who shrugged. She had a look on her face that I was beginning to realize was not the resignation I'd seen there so often before. She actually looked...intrigued. She held my arm, and we followed along behind Ken. Shawn stood by me on the other side. I think he was afraid I'd fall over. I was too, when it came down to it. Often, I simply felt overwhelmed. I hoped to heaven that there wasn't a crowd on the other side of Ken's front door waiting to yell "surprise."

I looked at Shawn then, feeling that apprehension, and realized he understood. He nodded his head toward the inside and gave my shoulder a reassuring pat. I let out the breath I'd been holding and stepped inside.

Even if there wasn't anyone yelling surprise, Ken's house was certainly surprising. It had been thoroughly and completely cleaned. The wooden floors had been sanded and refinished, and the walls were painted a creamy beige. The trim was as yet untouched, but the clutter was gone and the place smelled almost fresh and clean.

As we stepped farther in, I could see that the kitchen cabinets had been given a fresh coat of white enamel and that the appliances were new. As I followed Ken around his house, I was amazed by the changes he'd made. Each bedroom was immaculate and contained a bed, a club chair, and a small dresser. Although there was no furniture in the rest of the house except a small table and two chairs in the kitchen, it was obvious he'd gone to a great deal of trouble to make it habitable.

I had to admit it was really nice. If anything, I didn't understand why he'd brought us here. He seemed to be waiting for me to say something.

"Ken, you've made tremendous progress," I said. It sounded lame, even to me.

"I had a lot of help. I think at one point or another everyone in town was here."

"Congratulations." I looked at my mother and then back at him. "Small towns can be like that."

"So," he said. He was shifting from one foot to the other awkwardly. He seemed to be waiting for something.

"I'm really amazed, Ken. You are a very lucky man. I'm so grateful to you for bringing my mother to St. Nacho's from the airport." I paused, but the silence continued uncomfortably. "I'm really tired, Ken. Do you think Shawn could take us to the SeaView now?"

Ken looked at me like he didn't understand. "But I want you to stay here."

"What?" I looked to where my mom was standing. "My mother will be staying with me, so it's best if we're at the SeaView. I'm sure you understand. She doesn't want to go home until she's sure I'm not going to fall down in front of a bus or something."

"I want you and your mother to stay here," Ken said, implacably. "Together."

"I'm sorry, Ken. I think that would be a little uncomfortable. I'm really tired. Please. Can I just go home now?"

Ken sighed, stepping toward me so he could touch my hand with his. He lowered his voice and spoke gently to me. "Jordan. I don't plan on staying here. I'm going home to my parents' house. I just want you and your mother to be comfortable." He began to walk to the front door, turning back before he walked through it. "Shawn and Cooper brought your things from the motel. Your mom's cases are in the guest bedroom; yours are in the master. I put food in the fridge, and the phone works." He pulled open the door and was out of it before either my mom or I could say anything.

"Jordan," my mother said.

"I'm on it." I went after him. I made it to the porch just as he was getting in his car. "Ken!" I got his attention. He stood with the car door open in his hand.

"What?"

"Thank you so much for this. For everything." I wanted to get it all out. "For bringing my mother here. You don't know what a difference you've made. You can't know how much—"

"That was mostly Izzie's doing." He looked away. "I just did the house faster than I thought I would in order to give you someplace to go when you got out of the hospital."

"I hope to hell you know I wish everything were different. I wish we could figure out how to make things work—"

Ken interrupted me. "My batting coach at school used to say that wishing was like pissing. Everyone did it, but the results just go down the drain. He told me when you really want to hit the ball, you've got to have the courage to step up to the plate and face some motherfucker who's going to throw a hard ball at you—at a hundred miles per hour—and you have to *know* you're going to hit it before it even leaves his hand. I can't say I'm thrilled that you only *wish* we could figure out how to make it work between us."

"Ken—"

He grinned at me. Oh, holy crap, what a smile. *What a man.* "But I can't say I'm prepared to give up, either." He tossed his canes in ahead of him, got into his car, and drove off. My heart did a kind of twist thing in my chest that made it feel as though it had wrenched free of the pipes that kept it connected and pumping my blood.

"He seems to be a rather interesting young man," my mother said right behind me.

"You heard all that?"

"Yes I did." She put a hand on my arm and pulled me gently back inside. "Which is the master bedroom? I want you to lie down."

"Mother," I said, but she paid little attention. I exchanged glances with Shawn, who smiled his own perfect smile and shrugged. He took my arm and led me back down the hallway.

"I'm going to make something for us to eat when you wake up," my mother called from the kitchen. I didn't answer. I sat down on the bed, and Shawn stood in the doorway looking at me with what I thought was uncertainty. He had his hand in his jacket pocket as though he was toying with something. I waited.

"When you were in River Falls, you *hit* Cooper," he said, finally.

Somewhere along the line I'd learned that if I didn't want to look someone in the eye that probably meant I should. I nodded. "Yes, I did."

"When I saw your mother"—Shawn motioned to the side of his face—"I realized you probably got that from your home."

It was hard to get used to his uninflected voice, but I didn't find it displeasing. He pulled his hand out of his pocket, and I saw he had a phone with him. Two, if you counted the one that he had clipped to his belt.

He expected me to talk about this with him. I didn't think I had much of a choice when he came back into the room and handed me his spare phone. "Speed-dial pound sign one," he said. "I like Ken. I don't want to see him get hurt."

I figured out how to text. *You're right, and nothing I say should matter.*

After a minute or two, when his phone beeped, he read what I'd sent. "Say it anyway." He looked up. "Why shouldn't I tell Ken you hit my lover?"

*You should,* I typed. *You definitely should.*

"Why?" he asked, his fine brown eyes clearly baffled.

I thought about it. I typed, *One, it can't be a secret*, then pressed Send. I continued typing until I had sent two more messages. *Two, I have learned a hundred ways to manage anger without violence.* And, *Three, I have no more lies to protect. I don't want them.*

I looked up and watched as he digested this. "Why should I believe you've changed?"

I shook my head and typed, *You shouldn't. Nobody should. But I have.*

Shawn was silent for a long time. It wasn't hard to see why Cooper loved him so much. He was intelligent and finely made. He had a beautiful smile and, I suspected, an equally beautiful heart.

"Cooper's heart was very dark when I met him." He leaned against the wall. "He needed a good hard shove into the light, and I knew I was just the man to do it." He grinned.

I looked down, trying not to laugh. *How did you know?*

Shawn headed back toward the bedroom door. "He came like a train whenever I shoved him. He just had to accept that I had his best interest at heart. I love him."

I did laugh at this, out loud. I typed, *Good call, you're both very lucky.*

"You're lucky too." Shawn took a last look around the freshly painted bedroom. "Try not to overthink it."

*I need time*, I typed.

"Fair enough," he said simply and then caught the phone neatly when I tossed it to him. He turned to walk through the door, and I slumped over to lie down on the fully made bed, too exhausted to even worry about it. Shawn came back in and removed my shoes, actually picking me up halfway so he could pull the quilt out to cover me. As he left the room at last, he shot back over his shoulder, "It wouldn't kill you to learn some ASL, you know."

I grinned even as I began to drift off.

* * *

What I didn't tell my mother, what I wasn't telling anybody, was that the dream where I walked to River Falls with the flashlight was something that visited a lot. Not nightly, not exactly, but it came often and left me shaken and drenched with sweat. That night I woke at three a.m., terrified that I'd been loud and my mother would come rushing into my room. I looked at the clock by the bed. Thoughtful, *thoughtful* Ken, how like him to make sure I had a clock if I needed it. There were soft towels in the bathroom and crisp linens on the bed. I didn't have to think about soap or shampoo or toothpaste or toilet paper. The kitchen was full of food that was easy to prepare but good, like cheese and avocados for sandwiches, cans of vegetarian soup, and several different kinds of yogurt.

There was no way I would find sleep again, so I got up and went to the kitchen, where I rummaged around absently for food. I was making myself a cup of herb tea when my mom came in.

"Hi." It seemed so strange for us to be here together. It was completely uncharted territory. When I'd last been home, we had gotten together furtively so that I could practice massage techniques, yet here she was at the kitchen table with all the time in the world to chat, and now that we could talk freely we didn't have that much to say. "Want some? It's called 'Tension Tamer'; it's a little...lemony," I said, smelling it.

"Yeah, thanks," she told me. She was wearing a pair of flannel pajama bottoms with a long-sleeved T-shirt. She sat at the table, and I noticed she was braless and wondered when the last time was that I'd seen her in her nightclothes. Maybe I was about fifteen. Even then, I couldn't say that beyond my sorrow for her and the anger I felt that she let my dad abuse her, that I'd ever seen her as a *person*.

First, she'd been my mother, and then... Maybe I hadn't wanted to see her as someone like me. Someone whose dreams had come to an unbearable end. Her acceptance of my father's abuse made me angry. She had relaxed here in California; she came out of her room a lot more than I remember her doing when I was young. It was a sure sign she felt comfortable here.

I set a mug of tea down in front of her on the table, along with a spoon. There was a sugar bowl on the table, along with salt and pepper and a little rack with napkins in it. *Ken again.* My mother must have been thinking along the same lines.

"The young man who owns this house," she began. "He seemed to care very much about you."

I sat down with her and put sugar in my tea. "We hardly knew each other before I was hurt. He's a very nice guy."

She glanced around. "Yes, that would explain it. All nice guys go to this kind of trouble for perfect strangers."

"I can hardly be called a 'perfect' stranger."

"Tell me what happened, Jordie," she insisted.

I ran my hands through my hair, wincing as they ran over the scabs from where the staples had been removed. I picked up my tea. "Nothing happened. His mother warned me off. His brother hates me, hates him for being gay. He deserves someone better."

"Does he think that?"

"Did anyone tell you how he got like that? He was hit by a drunk driver. His best friend was in the car with him and she didn't make it. His mother thinks he's trying to recover by 'fucking the boogeyman.'"

"Jordan!"

"Give it a rest, Mom. I'm almost thirty; I doubt I'll stop saying fuck."

"That's not what I was going to say." Her lower lip quivered, and again I realized that I'd probably never really looked closely at her. Her eyes shimmered. "I was going to say that sometimes when you think you have everything all figured out, it goes to hell anyway. I was going to say that you can marry the person that everyone tells you is the perfect catch and still get it all wrong. I was *going to say* that you and Ken need to decide who is having this relationship, because the people who are telling you what to do aren't the ones who matter."

That was probably the most she'd said to me about relationships during my whole life.

I whispered, "You can't go back to him."

A single tear slipped down her cheek. "I don't want to go back, but so far I haven't figured out how to stay."

## Chapter Nineteen

I enjoyed working out-of-doors on Ken's yard, and as soon as I could, I spent the better part of my afternoons outside. In the week since I had moved into Ken's house, the weather had been cool and crisp and the days overcast. I'd discovered some tools in a dilapidated garden shed and was setting up in the backyard when the sun unexpectedly emerged from the blanket of clouds that so often shrouds St. Nacho's. I was particularly enjoying the way it felt on my back as I worked on weeding and edging the planters. At one point the garden must have been very nice; some of the flower beds were raised and the largely clay soil had been turned and amended with organic material. Still, a lot of it was packed and slabby, like someone had given part of the yard a go and worked it, but stopped before the whole thing was done. I could see myself here. Taking the time to perfect it one square foot at a time, making it beautiful again, for Ken.

I had a wheelbarrow and was adding garden soil and compost to the areas that had completely dried since the last rain, the parts that got the most sun, and cultivating the soil to get it ready for planting. I didn't know what Ken had in mind, but getting the flower beds ready seemed like something I could do, whatever he planned to plant there. I was dumping a small load of fresh, loamy soil onto one of his raised beds when I heard him clear his throat behind me.

"Hi." He looked at the ground where I was using this ingenious corkscrew-shaped claw to dig the new soil into the hard-packed clay. "You're not supposed to be working that hard."

I pushed the tool into the ground and turned, grimy from head to toe and covered with dirt, which stuck to the sweat on my forearms. I resisted the urge to wipe my brow and make everything worse. "I like this kind of work."

He smiled and took off the baseball hat he wore, balancing on his canes while he looked around. "You shouldn't overdo, whether you like it or not."

I shrugged. "It's going to be a nice yard in the spring."

"I feel a little guilty now; I bought the place for a song, and before escrow even closes it will be worth a lot more than I paid for it."

"Didn't you say the family that owned it doesn't live around here?"

"Yes, they're in Virginia. It was a headache for them, and it's not like St. Nacho's has San Francisco housing prices or demand."

"Are you seriously going to live here?" I led him back toward the house with the idea that I'd get cleaned up and maybe see if he wanted lunch. "In St. Nacho's? Your brother seems to think you've lost your ambition. There's more to baseball than playing. Have you thought of a different kind of career in the sport?"

"No."

"Why not? You could coach, get a job at your old university; there's umpire school in Florida—"

"I meant no, I haven't thought about it. Not that I wouldn't do it." He brushed past me when I opened the slider to the kitchen and then waited until I came into the house to continue. "I haven't thought that far ahead for any reason, except to buy this house. I wanted to share this house with you. That's the first...probably the only thing I've really wanted since the accident."

"That seems a little...precipitate." I went to the sink to scrub my hands and arms. I probably should have taken a shower, but I was strangely reluctant to shatter the moment. He was in a talkative mood, and my mother was out. It was the first time we'd had an opportunity to be alone since my attack. I sat across the kitchen table from him.

"No more than anything else," he remarked. "Tell me why you came to St. Nacho's."

"I—" *Why had I come?* "It's a long story. When I was in prison, I met this man who had a prison ministry." I wondered if that's where it started, or even if I understood my life myself enough to explain it. "He was nice, his name was Stan, and he helped me to find work and a place to live when I got out."

"Was he from California?"

"No, I went back to my hometown and then I called Cooper and he came back home too. I had this idea that we could... Well. The thing is, while I was in prison Stan kept talking about the love of the Lord, you know? He kept telling me how when I was worthy of it, I would feel so good, and all my problems would disappear or grow insignificant."

"Yeah?"

"Yeah, well. I was pretty eager to do whatever anyone said if it would make me feel better. I wanted to feel that love he kept talking about. I wanted to feel like I was working toward getting free of the guilt. He worked so hard at making me into the perfect little convert. I about killed myself to be everything he said I should be and I—"

"Did you love him?"

"No, it wasn't like that at all. He's a good man, and I guess I let him tell me how I should act because I wanted this idealized world he offered me. He just wanted to see me settle in a righteous life. It wasn't long before I stressed out trying to be perfect. I'm afraid that even while he was trying to make me into a saint, a part of me knew it was all a lie. I used to go to this BDSM club in the Twin Cities where I could scene with people. At the time I thought of it like a fast track to redemption. I let them punish me because I was sure I needed it, and it made me feel good. Sadly, better than religion."

"Punish you?" Ken's brows drew together. "Punish you how?"

"Bondage. Spanking. Whips. Canes. Doms brought me to a transcendent pain state, where I let go of all my questions and just... I melted away from everything. I can see now that it was just another drug, but at the time, I thought I needed it. I thought it was helping to make myself worthy."

"Jeez." Ken looked at his hands.

"It's an oversimplification, but what I learned from all that was that if I wanted to feel that love that Stan was talking about, I had to be prepared to offer it to others." Ken said nothing. I wondered what I expected. I sounded nuts, even to myself. "I chose to work in a field where I can help people, and I spend every day, pretty much, giving as much as I can. And it's worked. I used to live beneath a crippling guilt and now...I just live."

"So that's good, right?"

"Yes...it is. And no. I don't know. You came along and wanted to give me something, and I realized... I don't think I know how to accept kindness anymore. I'm afraid to take, afraid it will lead to selfishness or forgetting what's important." I guess I got angry when Ken started to laugh. "What the hell is so funny?"

"You are," he told me. "You're funny. You've probably got the warmest heart of anyone I've ever met. I'm drawn to you because I was freezing from loneliness and anger and it's like putting my hands near a fire."

"Me?"

"Yes, you." Ken slid his chair around the table toward mine and put his hands in front of me, close but not touching. "How can you not know this?"

"Ken, I'm a very selfish person; I have to watch everything I do, every day so that I don't backtrack."

"You still think you need rules to follow or you'll fuck up again?"

Maybe he was right. "I—"

"It's not rational, but I think you care for me, and being with you is like falling into the softest, most welcoming chair at the end of a long, hard day."

"Your parents will never let you—"

His eyes grew troubled. "I don't need my parents to *let* me do anything. If nothing else, I'm a grown man."

I was still looking down at the table when his voice cracked over me like a whip. "*Jordan.*" I raised my eyes to his. "If you need someone to tell you what to do, then let it be me."

"I—"

He leaned in. "You think too much. Trust me to know what I want. Trust yourself to give it to me if it's what you want too." He hooked his hand around my neck and squeezed, not hard, but just enough to let me know that he could control me through sheer physical power if he needed to, and fuck, I wanted to melt into his arms and let him. "Trust that I see you in a way that you can't see yourself."

I whispered, "I'm afraid of losing focus."

"Do you want me?"

I looked into his eyes and they were that warm violet-blue color they turned when I gave him pleasure. " *Yes.*"

His lips came down on mine, and I clung to his shoulders, stroking them with the palms of my hands, reveling in the thickness, the definition of the muscles under my fingertips. I went to him so abruptly that my chair fell over behind me. He stood with me and my head spun, so I let him lift me, teetering, and wrapped my arms and legs around him.

Ken tottered for a minute, then pushed me back against the nearest wall so he could balance and still support my weight.

"Sorry." I laughed against his neck. "I always forget we'll tip over if—"

"You have more faith in me than I do." He pulled my arms from around his neck and held them over my head while pinning me neatly to the wall with his body. "You don't just *like* this," he ventured. "You need this, don't you?"

I felt my face flush and couldn't meet his eyes. "What?"

"You didn't leave that life—the scenes—behind, did you? You respond like nothing I could have imagined when I—"

"Yes," I hissed. "Hell yes. I'm wired that way, all right? I *like* it." I stuck my chin up, afraid of what he'd say. "I've never had an intimate relationship where my quirks came into play, I've always kept it separate and almost clinical, but...yes."

"Do you want one?" he asked. "I don't mind telling you, I have an answering kink."

I wanted to die. "This is so embarrassing. I'm really not good at this sort of thing. I don't know how to do relationships. Can't you just fling me up against the wall like this when you want me and be done with it?"

Ken laughed and then shook his head. "For a little guy, you sure can be a lot of—"

"Who are you calling a little guy?" I demanded.

"Jordan, look at me," he commanded, and I did. The voice he used flowed through me like water. It was quiet and earnest, yet so powerful I could feel my body changing even as he spoke. "I know you think you can't trust what we feel."

"That's not true. I just—"

"You said as much at Izzie's, before the attack. You said you were the first out gay man I'd met, that I was responding to you because of the years I suppressed my sexuality."

"I didn't mean that the way you took it." I tried to move my arms, but he held them fast. "I didn't mean to imply you don't know what you want."

"Sure you did." He glowered at me, and I glared right back. "I don't know *everything* I want, Jordan, but I know I want you."

I lowered my eyes so he wouldn't see what that made me feel. I wanted to shout, *Fuck yes*, but I couldn't let the doubt go.

"I'm not going to ask anymore." He continued to hold me, his incredible upper body strength—both comforting and a little frightening—was something I could push against but never be free of unless he chose to allow it. Giving Ken power over me was a revelation. Surrender to him was *electrifying*. Sexy, but it also held the promise of immense comfort if I trusted him and allowed him to exercise that kind of control over me. "If you need someone to tell you what you want, please, let that someone be me."

I wanted it so badly I went rigid. "I'm afraid."

"Of me?" He brushed his lips against mine.

"Of...everything." It was true. I *was* afraid of everything; of losing my focus, of breaking the rules, of living for myself and harming someone again. I was afraid of any choice I made that didn't directly result from selfless service. Something I could understand and perform without faltering and failing people I cared about. "*I'm afraid of fucking up again.*"

"I've got you." He expelled a breath next to my ear that ruffled the hair there, and I pushed forward, into him, into the strength of his arms and the lure of being controlled by a strong, good man. "*I've got you.*"

I heard a car pull up outside, even as I watched the passion spark in Ken's eyes. When he heard my mother use the key in the front door, he let me slide down the wall, backing away from my body and letting me know with his eyes that he wasn't through with me *at all*. He sat back down at the table, and I walked to the refrigerator where I could get a grip on myself and find the makings for some sandwiches.

I stared at the shelves in the fridge for a minute as Izzie and my mother came into the room. My entire childhood was in that refrigerator: mayo and mustard, tomato, lettuce, and pickles. A number of different cheeses and lunch meats, big bowls of Jell-O and three-bean salad. I could hear that my mother was happy from her voice, and it made me smile. If nothing else, St, Nacho's was bringing her to life in a way I never expected.

"So, what do you think? Everyone loved the pie I made," my mother chirped proudly. "Oh, hi, Ken, nice to see you again. Is Jordan fixing you some lunch?"

I told her I was, and invited them to join us. Izzie was giving Ken and me a piercing look; I had no doubt at all that she knew exactly what she'd interrupted. "So. Settling in here nicely, I see."

I'm sure I looked guilty. "It's very good of Ken to let us stay here. I don't think it will be as long as the doctor imagines, I'm probably ready to start—"

"Nothing doing." Izzie stopped me. "If you even try to do an end run around doctor's orders, I will fire you on the spot."

I sputtered a little but in the end, I just made sandwiches. The four of us ate and talked, and if I noticed at the time that both Ken and my mother were less talkative than usual, it seemed only to be in contrast to Izzie, who more than made up for any deficit in the conversation. When Izzie and Ken got ready to leave, I wasn't sorry; they'd exhausted me.

Ken pulled me aside as he was about to follow Izzie out the front door and leaned in, brushing his lips to mine and pressing his lean, unshaven cheek against my temple as though he didn't want to let me go.

"Have faith, Jordie," he whispered. "I can be strong enough for both of us."

I searched his face then, not understanding exactly what he meant. His blue eyes held such warmth that I lost myself in them for a minute. I wanted to tell him he was; that he'd always been strong enough. I started to say something, my focus entirely on him, barely noticing when my mother cleared her throat and put a hand to my back, nudging me to let him go. He winked at me and left through the front door with a spring in his ungainly step that hadn't been there before, even though he still used two canes.

After he left, my mother went back toward the kitchen, muttering under her breath, "Like a couple of teenagers—at your age."

Absurdly, in my imagination I heard the Darlene Love song, "Today I Met the Boy I'm Gonna Marry," and it made me feel like I'd been hit over the head all over again.

* * *

Given how we'd left the subject open, it was a surprise when a week passed during which I didn't hear from Ken. Izzie, Andy, my Red Hat ladies, Cooper, and Shawn came by every day, in some combination of what I was beginning to think of as a vast conspiracy to convince me that the world was really a better place than I'd ever imagined it could be.

My mother was pink-cheeked and happy and had turned her hand to making pies for everyone as a way of saying thank you. She put the word out that anyone who brought over a pie plate could come back the following day and find it filled with something delicious, and she made good on her promises, even drafting me into the process when she found herself staring at a minuscule kitchen table stacked with fourteen pie plates. She and I looked at each other, and I don't know who thought it first, but suddenly we both knew how she could stay here, if she had the courage.

"Pie," she began, as though thinking out loud, "isn't a terribly expensive thing to make."

I didn't want her to get ahead of herself. "There are probably a million rules about how things have to be made, what the ingredients need to be, where you can and can't make it."

Her brows drew together. "Don't Cooper and Shawn work for a restaurant?"

"Yes. They do." I felt my heart begin to beat faster. "They serve a pretty extensive brunch on Sundays."

"Do people like pie at brunch, I wonder?" she asked.

"I don't know. But guests might want to take one home after a nice meal out. For later."

"I'll bet they like cinnamon rolls."

"Oh my G—"

"Don't take the Lord's name in vain, Jordie," she admonished automatically.

"But I just remembered your cinnamon rolls."

"Only now?" I could tell she was insulted.

"Mom, I don't remember much from when I was a kid," I admitted. I picked up a couple of the pie plates and looked at them. They were from a famous chain of pie restaurants where the pies were nowhere near as good as my mother's.

Out of the blue she said, "I'm so sorry, Jordie. I didn't do a great job of picking your father."

I really *saw* her right then, and she didn't look like my mom. She looked like one of my Red Hat ladies or my customers or my friends. She looked like any number of people I'd met in rehab. She looked like a nice lady, and I wanted to get to know her because I realized *I had no clue.*

We went to work in Ken's tiny, well-scrubbed kitchen, getting out the ingredients for her specialty, apple-pecan pie. She made the pie dough with such a sure hand it boggled my mind. She was rolling it and dropping it into pie shells, fluting the edges so they looked like the pies on a magazine cover. I turned on music, and while we peeled apples and made her custard fillings, she let loose and danced a little.

It was the first time I'd ever seen my mother happy like that, hopeful and confident, and I hated to admit what I might do to see to it that she stayed that way. We went to bed that night after all the pies were picked up and exclaimed over. The following day I was going to see if Cooper would come with me to talk to Jim, the owner of Nacho's Bar. Maybe we could pick his brain about how to start a small bakery business in town. I knew there was a lot to think about, a lot to learn. I knew there would be money involved and maybe more than we could come up with. But when my mother went to bed that night, I could see that for once she wasn't unhappy or afraid. Nothing else mattered to me but that.

# Chapter Twenty

I had the dream again. It was taking its usual course; I was walking across the heartland clothed in nothing but a hospital gown, but that wasn't what woke me up. A staccato noise began to invade the dream itself, and I woke, startled, to realize it came from the window of my bedroom. I listened for a minute, thinking I was mistaken, but the sound, sharp and insistent, came again. There were no curtains, and I could see someone was out there, tapping a fingernail on the glass.

When I got closer, I made out Mark's face and motioned for him to meet me around at the back door. I tried to go quietly through to the kitchen but heard my mother's sleepy voice.

"Jordie? Is that you?"

"Yeah," I answered just outside of her bedroom door. "It's nothing, Mom, go back to sleep. Ken's little brother is here, probably playing a prank or toilet-papering the house or something."

"Tell him he's cleaning it up if he does. No pie for him," she murmured, and I grinned. As I walked away I heard her chuckle. "He shall have *no* pie."

I opened the back door and let him in. "Do you have any idea what time it is?"

"I want you to come with me."

"Where?" I asked. "Can't this wait until morning?"

"No, it has to be now." He bit his lip. "I want you to see something. My friend Katy brought her car so we can go, but we have to go *now.*" I locked the back door behind him and led him toward the front. I was wearing flannel drawstring pants and a T-shirt. There wasn't anything wrong with them; if I wanted I could wear them outside. He followed as I went to the front to get a jacket out of the coat closet. From the look of him, wearing jeans, a flannel shirt, and a down vest, his cheeks stained pink and his hair damp, I thought it was probably a little crisp. I pushed my feet into a pair of canvas shoes I kept by the front door.

"Is this going to be okay?"

"You're fine," he said. "Just come with me."

I closed and locked the front door behind me. I didn't leave a note, but Mark was in such a hurry that I just reacted. An older-model white Mazda was parked at the curb, and by the interior light I could see a pretty girl sitting inside, putting on lip gloss. She was a wonderful creamy brown color, with a mane of thick, curly hair. She turned when she saw us, and I saw that she had a pretty face, high cheekbones, tip-tilted eyes, and full, now shiny, lips.

"This is Katy," Mark said, without the kind of reverence she should have inspired in a boyfriend. "She's a friend from school." I got into the front seat after he tilted it forward and slid into the back.

"What are we doing?" I finally asked. There was a rhythm to my life these days that didn't include being kidnapped by high school children.

"I want you to see something," Mark said. He didn't elaborate.

"Is it bigger than a bread box?" I asked, and Katy giggled.

"Ken's been sneaking out at night, and I followed him to see where he's been going. He's really starting to worry me."

I frowned. "It isn't right to invade his privacy, Mark. If he's going out at night, he has that perfect right."

Even after the last time I'd seen him, when I thought we'd settled at least that we wanted each other, even after his declarations, I was afraid that whatever Ken was doing in the middle of the night wasn't something *I* wanted to see. Whatever he was up to was his business, but what my mind conjured, Ken fucking rent boys up against alley walls or Ken meeting a lover to have sex on the beach, bothered me far more than I was prepared to admit. I didn't believe it of him, but in my heart I was afraid that I'd misjudged him. I shook myself out of it. If Ken needed me, for whatever reason, I was there.

"I'm worried about him," Mark reiterated. "He works out with free weights constantly and only leaves the house for therapy. Pull over here, Katy," he told his friend. She did what he asked, turning the car engine and the lights off about a block and a half away from Nacho's Bar. "Then I realized he was slipping out at night."

I sighed. "Look, when your brother came out, I know how hard that was for you. I know how disappointed you were. But for a lot of reasons, you can't be following him around. He has a right to a life of his own. Who he sees, whatever their gender, has nothing to do with you."

He looked past me like he wasn't listening at all. "Just get out, okay? I need to show you." We all got out of the car and stood for a minute. I looked to Mark for instructions. He motioned I should follow him. "Come with me."

We started off walking, and although I didn't have my watch on, I knew it had to be about three or four in the morning. Nacho's was closed up tight. The only light came from the streetlamps, shrouded in fog, and the moon, which showed the barest hint of something orb like illuminating the clouds from behind.

I followed Mark until we reached the boardwalk, watching as he rather dramatically slipped along next to the Nacho's building in its shadow. When we got to the edge of the bar, he crouched low and crept to the sea wall, hiding behind it.

I followed silently, as did Katy, doing just as he did. The first thing I noticed was what I thought might be a mound of sand on the beach in the distance by the water's edge. As I watched, it shifted and hunched, and I realized there was a person lying there. I started to say something, but Mark put his hand out to stop me and hissed.

"Shh," he said barely above a whisper. "Sound carries in fog."

That it did. What I could now clearly see was a man, groaning as he lifted himself first to all fours, and then, staggering, upright. He took one step, agonizing and awkward, and then another. He got about four or five yards down the beach and fell again to begin the whole process over. I looked at Mark.

"He leaves the canes over by his car with his coat," he mouthed. "He just walks down there for hours. Every night."

"Jeez."

"He's trying to get stronger, working himself until almost dawn," Mark said under his breath. "He's pushing himself so hard—"

"Shh." Katy put a reassuring hand on his arm. She looked at me. "Can you help?"

I turned and sat down on my ass with my back to the sea wall. "I don't know." Mark's hair was blowing in the breeze, and his resemblance to Ken was haunting. "I'm not sure. He obviously doesn't want us to know he does this."

I looked back over the wall behind me to see that Ken had fallen again. He rose, dragging himself upright by sheer force of will, I thought, and moved forward again. It was breaking my heart to watch him. I not only felt for him, but I was aware that this was like peering into and speculating about the most intimate details of his life. He wouldn't thank any of us for seeing this.

"You have to do something. It's killing him. Watch." Mark jerked his head, and I looked on as Ken once again struggled to his feet. He did this several more times, each time more gut-wrenching than the one before it, and finally, I could see, even hear, that he lay facedown on the sand shaking with sobs.

"Every night?" I asked.

"Every. Single. Fucking. Night." Mark bit off each word as though he were yanking the pin from a grenade. He looked at me. "Somebody has to stop this. I think... *I believe* it has to be *you*. I think he loves you."

If it were possible, I felt myself shrink just a little more. *He told me he would get strong enough for both of us. Is this what he meant?*

"You need to go talk to him. You need to stop him from hurting himself." Mark's eyes were wide in his face. I knew he was right. Somebody had to stop Ken. What he was doing wasn't only ill-advised, but by not sleeping he was using up resources that he needed to heal. That was common sense.

"Go home," I told Mark and Katy. "Call my mom and tell her I had to leave to help a friend. She'll be worried when she wakes up if I'm not there, and I didn't leave a note."

Mark nodded. He and Katy started to crawl back to the shadows of Nacho's Bar, but he turned back to me. "Look. I'm sorry I got so—"

"Go home," I told him again. "We'll talk more later." I watched as they disappeared around the back of the building heading for Katy's car.

I slipped off my shoes and left them on top of the sea wall. Except for being cold, I enjoyed the way the sand slipped under my feet. I could see why Ken was using it to exercise. It was challenging. It worked all my muscles and kept me fighting for balance as it shifted and slid beneath me.

I wasn't being exactly stealthy when I walked across that sand, and I knew that Ken could hear me. He didn't look up, and I thought he might have been pretending to sleep, hoping whoever was coming wouldn't bother him. As I got closer and still got no reaction, I became concerned and dropped to my knees beside him.

"Ken?" I put a hand on his back. He jerked back, gasping in a big breath of air. He *had* fallen asleep, exhausted. He looked at me with round, confused eyes, and I just slipped down beside him and took him into my arms.

"What? What're you—"

"Shh," I whispered.

"How did you find me?"

I debated how much to tell him. "Magic."

"Mark." He sighed. "I thought he was looking tired lately. I should have recognized the signs. So…neither of us has been getting any sleep."

"He's very worried about you." I pulled him so he rested with his back tight against my chest.

After a while he said, "It's no use."

"What?"

"I'm not going to get a whole lot better." He was staring out at the ocean, spooned up against me, and I felt his body tremble a little.

"Maybe you're not," I said. "Maybe you are. I don't know. You're strong, though, Ken. Plenty strong enough for whatever you need. For whatever I need."

"I thought I could come down here and walk on the sand—you know, like Rocky or something—like all I would need is the will, if I just want it badly enough."

"That only works in the movies because they're an hour and a half long. Your recovery could take a year or more. You're not giving yourself enough time."

"I wish we'd met before the accident."

"Why, so I could have been a one-night stand when your ball club played the A's? Think about it. You and I wouldn't have had a chance before. You wanted to stay in the closet, and I wasn't interested *in* or capable *of* relationships."

"Will you still want me even though I may never be the man I was?"

I pictured Ken's mother standing in front of me in the parking lot at Day-Use saying *cut him loose*. "Your mother has other plans for you."

"I can't worry about my mother." Ken shook his head. "I can only worry about my body, my attitude, my state of mind. My heart. Whether my muscles are strong enough or my balance is good enough. I can only worry about whether I'll ever walk without assistance again. I don't need to worry about my mother," he ground out. "She needs to worry about me."

"She *is* worried about you."

He sighed deeply and pushed back against me, pulling my arms tighter around him.

"She may be right, Ken. You may never have wanted someone like me if you hadn't had the accident. When you're better you may want to move on."

"That's true," he agreed, turning over to look me in the eye. "But I may not. And isn't that true of anyone you'd meet? Anyone I'd meet? You make me *feel* good."

I admit I might have smiled a knowing kind of smile.

"Not just that way." He pushed me onto my back. "But yeah, that way. I feel...like Goldilocks. This one is *just right.*"

"Me too."

"Yeah?"

"Yeah. Like being here now." I reached up and pushed some strands of hair off his face, but the wind blew them right back. "I should have been here for you all along. No skulking around trying to be all strong and shit." He looked away. "I don't care how well you get around. I just want to be by your side."

He leaned in for a kiss. "I want you."

"You have me."

He stilled. "How?"

*Was he asking to be reassured? How did he have me?* "However you want me. I'm yours. Wherever. Whenever. Whatever. I swear I'll stand by you. And if it all goes to hell or your family gives me shit? Bring it on. As long as you want me, I'm there."

He was still for so long I thought I'd said the wrong thing. Finally, he touched his lips to mine again, delicately, and I felt the tenderness seep through that kiss as he ran a hand down my back to my ass. He froze. "Are you in your *pajamas?*"

"Yeah, well, magic doesn't wait for you to dress," I said sourly.

"I'll work on our manners." He was feeling my ass with both hands, kneading the muscles there, and I could tell he was getting ideas.

"Your timing could be better too," I said, thinking that I didn't really want to be arrested for lewd acts on the beach at four in the morning. "I hope to fuck you'll give me a ride home, because I told Mark and Katy to go. I've got the mother of all headaches again, damn it."

"Sure; I'm parked by the pier." He began to haul himself to his feet, and I got to mine to help him. I got up too quickly, got dizzy, and stumbled for a minute and thought about what a dumbass pair we made, laughing a little.

"What?"

"It occurred to me that I might not be much use to you yet."

"Yeah." He grinned. "I wasn't going to say anything, but you're kind of a spaz."

"Pot, meet kettle. Kettle, pot."

"I want to walk back." He tightened his lips. "I'm not very good at it."

"Let's do it together. I'll be here if you need me." I looked toward the pier. "It's not like we have a choice."

He placed a hand lightly on my shoulder. "It's slow going."

"I've got time." I swallowed hard. "I swear to you there's no place on earth I'd rather be." He hooked his arm around my neck and pulled me to him again, his lips coming down hard on mine for a searing kiss. He framed my face with his hands and drew away. His eyes promised me that was only the beginning.

## Chapter Twenty-one

I don't know exactly how many times the dream of Bobby came again, visiting, knocking on the door of my sleeping self. It still came regularly after my car was found abandoned and burned on Interstate 80 just outside of Cheyenne, Wyoming. After my mother found a new life baking pies for six of the restaurants in town and a temporary place to live above Nacho's Bar. After I had healed and my hair had grown back—cropped close—almost completely hiding the scars. The dream kept coming even after Ken and I had been living together in his house for a time, spending our days working and our nights and weekends fixing and painting and gardening and making love.

Sometimes small details changed. I thought I was dreaming in order to relive the outcome of the tragedy and I was destined to have the same dream forever. So if it changed, even the smallest bit, I was surprised.

Then one night I dreamed that after waking in the hospital, I made my usual way out via the elevator onto the beach by Nacho's Bar. As always, I crossed over vast space in my hospital gown and ended up in River Falls. My hometown was dark and silent before me as I crossed familiar landscapes. When I went up to the door with the Johnson family knocker on it, I rapped three times.

Perfect, whole Bobby Johnson answered the door carrying a toy truck. I looked down at my hand, and predictably, I had the flashlight, but Bobby didn't scream when he saw me. Instead, he looked up at me with unblinking brown eyes. I held out my hand, the one that did not contain the flashlight, and he took it with his.

It seemed then as though I almost dreamed it all backward; River Falls was getting smaller and smaller behind us as we trudged across the farmlands and prairies together. In the distance I could just begin to make out the glittering, changeable Pacific Ocean. First we came to the high cliffs, where steep and rocky paths led down to the tidal pools, and then, our feet submerged, we stood in the shallow water, toes tingling from the cold.

Bobby Johnson, my dream Bobby, who always seemed so alive and whole, took my flashlight from me, casting it as far as he could out over the water. It landed with a satisfying *thunk* and disappeared into the churning green sea below. He looked at me again and then at the toy in his hand. He handed over the die-cast metal truck and looked serenely out to sea. I flung that truck twice as far as he'd thrown the flashlight, and when it hit the water, the sun seemed to set behind it, slipping into the fiery horizon until there was only a glowing burst of raw and vivid color left behind. I looked down to see how Bobby was taking that, if he thought it was as beautiful as I did, but he was gone.

I jerked awake.

"What is it?" Ken asked me when he felt me sit up.

"I had that dream again. It was…it was all wrong."

He slipped a hand around my hips and pulled me into that muscled body of his. "What do you mean?"

"I dreamed that this time, instead of Bobby screaming or running away, we came here, to St. Nacho's, and he threw the flashlight from my attack into the ocean."

"Yeah?" He sat up.

"Then he gave me a toy truck. I threw that away as well, and the sun set."

"Really?" He reached out an arm and pulled me to him so that I straddled his lap. I put my head down on his shoulder, in my favorite place, with my lips against his neck. "Do you think that means you got rid of it? The past?"

I tensed. "I hope not!"

"Why not?" he asked. "What good is carrying it around?"

"I can't let go of that. I can't. It's like saying it's okay. It would be like I'm okay with Bobby's death. As if I could *get over it.*"

Ken seemed to think this over. "Before, when things were tough and you were just starting over in a new life, I think you may have needed the guilt to keep you from making bad choices."

"Isn't *that* the understatement of the century?"

"You've been making good decisions ever since I've known you. You've done the right thing. You've helped others; been generous with your time. You're a good guy for kids like my brothers to look up to."

"Yes, but—"

"Maybe the dream is telling you it's time to let go of—"

"No!" I stopped him. "I *need* to carry him with me. If I stopped, that would be like killing him twice." I couldn't say why, but the idea of throwing away my past made me feel empty and terrified.

"I was going to say that maybe you should keep Bobby, keep the sorrow, keep the memory so that it can continue to guide you, but lose the guilt."

"How do you lose guilt?" I asked. I couldn't imagine. Every time I thought of Bobby a fresh wave of pain sluiced through me.

"Maybe…" He pulled me to him and began stroking circles on my back with the flat of his hand. "Maybe you should allow it to become a passion for helping others." It was so dark and quiet in our room that I could hear his gentle breathing and every slip of the sheets against his warm skin.

Suddenly his lips looked full and luscious by the light of the moon coming through the window. "Passion," I repeated.

"For helping others," he reminded me with a grin.

"Nobody else is up at this hour."

"That's true… So you're off the humanitarian clock?"

"Well, unless you can think of something *you* need done." I leaned in and kissed him, grinding on him a little until he definitely had something he needed done.

"Oh, yeah," he growled.

I leaned over to the nightstand we'd purchased at a garage sale and pulled lube and a condom out of the drawer. I turned my head sharply back because I thought I caught a glimpse of something golden and luminescent around him. Izzie was trying to convince me that it was his aura, that everyone had the capability of reading them, and that his was golden and shiny because he was happy. She told me we were still exactly in sync. That much, at least, seemed to be true.

Ken and I knew each other well enough now that we could fall together and practically glide into making effortless love. He knew my body better than I did, and I knew more than a few tricks with regard to his. It never needed more than the hint that he was ready, or I was, and we'd find each other and create that perfect space that was just ours.

He leaned me back and licked his way down to my navel. "*Yes.*"

His dark hair was stark against my skin in this light, even though I'd managed to get quite brown, for me, from our frequent walks on the beach. I no longer allowed him to go in the dead of night. Often Mark and his friends showed up for an impromptu game of volleyball or a fire in one of the cement rings.

He shifted me off him and slid down to take my balls in his mouth, suckling on them one at a time, dropping under them to let his tongue slip farther down behind until he breached my hole and made me gasp with pleasure. I was ashamed of how I moaned and begged, but it never stopped me. I rolled over to get more contact, drawing my knees under myself and spreading as far as I could go. He used his thumbs to pull my ass cheeks apart and moaned when he found what he was looking for, that leverage he could always use to make me do whatever he told me to do.

He pulled away, and I'm sorry to say I whimpered when I no longer felt his touch. He replaced his tongue with slick fingers and, at the same time, slapped my ass hard enough to leave a mark with the other hand.

"Guh." My face hit the pillow. "Oh *fuck*."

"Hands on the headboard." He always found a deep and masterful voice for this, and I loved him for it. He slapped my other ass cheek because I lay there panting too long. I knew for a fact that he could make me come just by slapping my ass and talking to me in the voice he was using right then.

"Yes." I put my hands on the headboard, wrapping them around the slats, and his hand came down on my ass again, so hard I felt my balls fly forward and slap back. "Yes!" *This* was why my mother couldn't live with us.

I heard him pick up the condom, then hesitate. "Jordan—"

"Glove up," I told him implacably.

"How many tests is it going to take?" he asked. "You've been negative how many times now? I've been negative twice since we've—"

"Until I'm ready."

"I want to lose the latex."

I turned my head to face him. Maybe it was telling that I didn't let go of the headboard. "I will not do anything that might endanger you."

"Jordan, you're clean. As far as anyone could possibly know, you're clean and so am I. Have you been with anyone besides me since we met?"

"Of course not, how could you even ask such a lame question?"

"Neither have I." He gripped my hip with one hand and flicked the condom over the side of the bed with the other. "You're clean."

"I'm not sure. I'm not ready." I felt like pleading. I didn't *feel* clean.

"You're clean," he told me, lining up and starting that push into my ass. "I'm clean and I need you," he panted. I turned back around and rested my forehead against the headboard. For the first time, it was a struggle, almost painful. "Let me in, Jordan."

"Oh, fuck, Ken." He stroked the skin along my back with his hand and pushed harder. "I don't *know*. I don't know if I can do this."

He put his hands on mine where they still gripped the slats and bit my shoulder in the fleshiest part by my neck, hard. "Let me in." He used the voice that made me see stars; I felt him sink into me as I shivered with need and pushed back. He kept his hands on mine as he used his powerful quads to rock us both.

I knew exactly what we must look like, his ass flexing and snapping as he fucked me, and me with my head hanging, my hands gripping, taking it and loving it, melting. The image of that powerful body covering mine always got my head in the game even before my body started its unstoppable slide into climax.

I felt my orgasm like a tight ball of energy that started in my spine and radiated down my legs and back up, and soon I was incoherent with pleasure, making some sort of howling sound as I shot. He was groaning and pushing me closer and closer to the headboard. As soon as I let myself go and shuddered against him, I felt him, hot and sticky, inside me, so slick it felt like we were flying.

We fell on our sides together, and he wrapped a possessive arm around my chest and pulled me back against him. I could feel his cum dripping out of my ass, and I *liked* it. I started to laugh softly, and I can never really remember when it turned into tears.

"Damn," he whispered. "I love you."

"Me too." I was snorting with laughter while tears were wetting the pillow. "Oh, *fuck you.* Me too."

# Epilogue

Everyone I knew was in the stands for the Fourth of July baseball game between the Narcs, the official team of the Santo Ignacio police department, and the Sparks, Santo Ignacio's firefighters.

A coin toss decided which team got to claim the town's very own unofficial secret weapon, Ken Ashton. Ken wasn't likely to play pro ball, ever, and we'd all felt the pain and bitter disappointment of that. He could still put on a suicide squeeze play or drop a sacrifice bunt on a Chiclet anywhere in the infield no matter who was pitching, and before every hometown game, a coin was tossed and the battle waged to get him on their team. This time, the coin toss went to the Narcs, who hated my suggestion that they wear T-shirts that bore the logo *N* for Narcs followed by SIPD for Santo Ignacio Police Department on them, but they acquiesced when they realized my mother's fledgling bakery business had not only paid for the shirts and placed a giant ad on the back, but would be providing after-game treats as well.

I'd long since gotten over that "Casey at the Bat" nervousness when they called Ken in to pinch-hit, always with the bunt in mind and always with runners on base. Of course, the opposition was determined to walk him before he even got off the bench these days, but when they had the bases loaded like today, they didn't have any choice but to pitch to him. He always took a practice swing in the on deck circle with a wolfish smile that frankly turned my insides to goo.

Andy, who was bearlike but fast, was limbering up to run for him if he got on base, but no one believed it would ever come to that. Getting on base wasn't his goal, so the fact that he rarely achieved it didn't bother him much. If there were fewer than two outs, he planned to advance the runners. Sometimes, though, with men on base late in a game, they put him on, even if there were two outs, because more than once he'd knocked a ball into the parking lot, and then he had all the time in the world to make his way around the bases. He no longer needed crutches or even a cane, but he had a pretty clear limp and his left foot dragged just a little. Sometimes he tripped and fell in a mass of man and muscle that was just plain hard to watch. I noticed his eyes always sought mine afterward, as if he found something there that made it all right.

Marty Flyfenster was on the mound for the Sparks. Marty was known by all to be a competitive hothead. He'd been roughed up for two base hits and given up a walk before Ken came up, and I could tell he was touchy and maybe getting a little wild. He had two outs and he was looking to make Ken the third so he could get out of the inning.

The first pitch was high and outside, and I thought he probably hadn't meant for it to be. The second swept so close to Ken's ear that my man had to hit the dirt. I was on my feet in an instant, but Ken, knowing that I wasn't the coolest-headed guy around when it came to him getting dusted off by an inside pitch, turned and waved me down again.

There was a lot of muttering in the stands around me, as we were clearly in the "everyone in this row LOVES Ken Ashton" section. My mother was sitting with Ken's mother, Lydia, having struck up a tentative friendship when Lydia realized the futility of hoping I would go away. Mark was sitting on my other side with his father and the rest of the Ashton siblings.

"No pie for you!" my mother barked at Flyfenster in a shockingly loud voice.

Everything would have gone on like nothing had happened if Flyfenster hadn't smirked when Ken got awkwardly back to his feet.

Whatever Ken had been planning, everything changed with that single quirk of Flyfenster's mouth. When the next ball came over the plate, low and over the outside corner, just perfect for Ken to golf right out to the Kentucky Fried Chicken franchise on the other side of the park, he pulled back and lined it right at Flyfenster's head. To his credit, Marty put a gloved hand up and knocked it down, grabbing it in short order to fist it to first. His throw was off, though, and he one-hopped it; it took a bad bounce and went past EMT Jason Lents, the first baseman, who I knew from my accident wielded a tiny flashlight better than a baseball glove. When Lents had to chase it, Ken looked wildly around him for some clue of what to do.

Everyone was screaming. We were, by now, all on our feet, and the noise was deafening around me. Instinct took over, and Ken put his head down, rounding first base and heading for second. First one run scored, and then a second, but the real drama was Ken tearing for second base as though his ass were on fire, trying to beat the tag. His body mechanics fought him all the way, but his nature, competitive and predatory, gave second baseman Mario Cruz, another EMT, something to think about as Ken dived all-out for the bag.

The ball left Lents's hand like a rocket as soon as he caught up with it and headed straight for Cruz's perfectly positioned glove. Jim from Nacho's Bar was there to call it. Dust flew everywhere, and when the collision took place, bodies audibly slammed together and cleats skidded along in the dirt. Cruz was shorter than Ken and stockier. For Ken it must have been like hitting a brick wall. I could see he got his hand in, under Cruz's glove, but I couldn't tell whether he'd beaten a tag. Whatever else happened, the momentum of his run caused his feet to fly up when his body was stopped, and they rolled together for a second like a cartoon fight in the dirt before everything came to a thudding halt.

Jim had to jump back out of the way, but threw his hands down, spreading them wide. "SAFE!" he screamed. The stands emptied, and even though it was only the fourth inning, for all intents and purposes the game was over. Lents and Cruz joined in on a dog pile of men and women on Ken, who required Steri-Strips on his chin where he split it open. One or two of the new NSIPD T-shirts got all bloody as the Narcs held them to Ken's face while someone ran for a first-aid kit. Cooper cranked up the PA system and started playing ZZ Top's "Decision or Collision," shooting me a wide grin and a thumbs-up sign.

Eventually all the chaos died down. I was sitting on the bench with Ken when Shawn and Cooper came over to give us plastic bowls of my mother's apple pie with ice cream on top. I said, "Thank you for the pie," to Shawn in ASL, and even though it wasn't exactly as though I'd recited the Gettysburg Address, he hugged me hard and sat down next to me like I was his new best friend.

Izzie and Andy stopped by and sat on the ground, each with their own bowls of pie. "Your mom is a genius." Izzie swirled her pie with her ice cream until it looked like mush. "She told me your dad filed for divorce. How is she taking that?"

"He tried to browbeat her over the phone. Told her that she owns whatever she had on her back and not to try to come back for anything else. Mom told him he had nothing she wanted, ever again. She's tougher than I thought."

"He has no right." She frowned. "There are laws…"

"I think my mom is getting a kick out of spitting in his face." I looked down at my pie, a new apple-cranberry my mother was calling Freedom Pie for the Fourth and, I suspected, for her own Independence Day. "I don't know if he'll let it end there; I'd be surprised if he did." If he did, it was because he was already moving on with someone else. There had always been women in town who found my dad attractive, even with all his faults, and he'd held that over my mother's head enough times for me to wonder if he hadn't made good his threat.

Cooper patted my arm. "If he tries anything, everyone in this town will stand against him; you know that."

I felt relieved because I did know that.

"They still match?" Andy asked Izzie, jerking a chin to let her know he was talking about Ken and me. "Their auras?"

"Like bookends," she said.

Andy laughed through his nose to keep from spewing his pie. Ken brought my hand to his lips and kissed it. I'd been paying so much attention to Ken, I didn't know what happened during the game. I don't think anyone cared too much what the outcome was after Ken's at bat.

"Do you know who won?" I asked Cooper, who automatically translated into sign language for Shawn.

Shawn laughed his odd laugh and signed something back. He looked at Ken, who had an arm wrapped possessively around my waist.

Cooper grinned. "Shawn says it looks like you did, Jordie."

## THE END

# Z. A. Maxfield

Z. A. Maxfield is a fifth generation native of Los Angeles, although she now lives in the O.C. She started writing in 2006 on a dare from her children and never looked back. Pathologically disorganized, and perennially optimistic, she writes as much as she can, reads as much as she dares, and enjoys her time with family and friends. If anyone asks her how a wife and mother of four manages to find time for a writing career, she'll answer, "It's amazing what you can do if you completely give up housework."

Check out her website at http://www.zamaxfield.com.